Cora's bumpy path to inner happiness

Cora's bumpy path to inner happiness

Published by The Conrad Press in the United Kingdom 2019

Tel: +44(0)1227 472 874
www.theconradpress.com
info@theconradpress.com

ISBN 978-1-911546-68-9

Typesetting and Cover Design by:
Charlotte Mouncey, www.bookstyle.co.uk

The Conrad Press logo was designed by Maria Priestley.

Printed and bound in Great Britain
by Clays Ltd, Elcograf S.p.A.

Cora's bumpy path to inner happiness

Nadine Hunter

To my best friend.
For your patience, love, calm and support.
Always.

1

At what age do we start to understand love, love in its full intensity and force?

Cora realised that she had spent most of her life in search of something magical, of dreams and fluffy expectations, like a small child not able to fall asleep on Christmas Eve for the excitement of what was to come.

And at fifty-two, part of her was still in search of that dream. But only a small part of her believed in that now. She had, far too often, followed her heart rather than the sensible voices coming from her head which, to a stranger, would make her sound rather naïve, but Cora was far from it. Her unfortunate choice of men, and her own personal attitude towards health (a profound hypochondria, in the form of cancer phobia, to be more precise), had handed her a life she had certainly lived to the full, but not often felt truly alive in.

She had experienced such highs, that only those who have had the luck to live them, know of those moments that take your breath and snatch it from deep within you, in such a way, that leave you with an explosion of utter bliss and joy like never before.

Lately though, Cora was starting to fear she might be turning into someone like Prince Charles in that ill-fated interview when he got engaged to Diana, and when asked by the reporter whether they were in love, he replied… 'whatever 'in love' means.'

Was she losing hope and making far too much of her memories and her past, rather than longing for a happy future?

Cora had truly been luckier than most, and she did feel grateful. She had experienced brief but extraordinary moments of passion and lust. Other relationships were based on deep friendship and companionship, which nowadays seemed to Cora generally a much better type of relationship.

But what now? What was awaiting her in the next phase of her life and, more importantly, what was she going to allow to travel through her veins and soul this time? She felt she had gone full circle.

During her three years with Sebastian, her last companion, her heart and soul had been thoroughly filtered and pushed through a colander, leaving only the very basics, the things that stick whatever the circumstances, like starch. There were none of the joyous flutterings, the dreamy imaginations of the evenings and days to come and the holidays to be shared.

She felt naked. At a time when naked was the last thing she felt she wanted to be. She was spending less time looking after herself which she resented, as that was one thing she had been good at. She didn't feel particularly fit or in shape. She had abandoned herself to eat those things she knew her body didn't really need but at the same time, gave her short-term relief, and a great deal of comfort. She avoided looking at herself in the mirror as much as possible. What truly mattered to Cora, was her continuous and strong love for her children and her adored dog, Skye.

Cora was well aware that her life had taken a certain direction which wasn't born out of ambition, dreams or great excitement, but one of quiet resignation on most days, and acceptable contentment on high ones.

Nothing else.

Well, not for the moment, at least. Cora knew the above, was far from what she really desired. With regards to her self-image, she respected herself too much to abandon looking after her body and looks completely, but it was just not a priority, not at the moment... in fact it had not been for the last few years...

Having remained pretty fit, and a good weight, up to her late forties, a little too much rich food and drink seemed to have replaced the will to go for a run every day, and to spend twenty minutes on the rowing machine before breakfast. Those healthy habits had taken a rather more erratic turn for the worse.

Food and drink had replaced the love of a man and become her full-time companions. Battling that constant, vague wobble on her thighs seemed so much, much harder now and even when she put everything into it for a couple of weeks or so, one weekend of a little over-indulgence made the effort seem just hopeless and hardly worth it.

Cora always looked upon those people who tell you they can eat anything, as they have a very fast metabolism, with a stab of jealousy and resentment.

Having said all that, she knew she was lucky to be pretty enough to be able to look reasonably good, if she made an effort, whatever her clothes may be hiding underneath.

During these last few years, Cora believed that although she had never taken her focus off loving her children to the full, Francis, Belle and Ludo, a small part of her longed for something more. Something that would take the edge off her loneliness, and she was sensing this more and more every day.

That Monday in early June, Cora had gone on a shopping spree for long and floaty dresses for the summer, trying them under those inevitably horrid and cruel lights that one only comes across in shops' changing rooms.

She closed her eyes while slipping things on to avoid catching the sight of her naked body in the mirror. She had a quick glance above her for cameras.

Had shopping for clothes, which she had adored doing all her life, lost its excitement and charm?

Cora had returned home, hung the oversized linen dresses up and looked at them like you would an old lover, whose looks had definitely faded over the years. They felt comforting but hardly sexy.

Cora still felt that, deep down, she was an attractive woman; with long blonde unruly hair, verging on the bohemian on its bad days, and long elegant arms and legs. She looked every bit a lady. And when she had moved into the village of Mollington, ten years before, the locals had certainly believed she was.

Cora had a certain air about her, an aura that couldn't go amiss. She came from a privileged background, where one might have assumed a certain degree of pomposity, but that was not who she was at all.

She reflected deep kindness, compassion and care whenever she spoke to anyone and reached out to people, even when she was feeling at her lowest.

Cora knew she was good at hiding her feelings from strangers.

Mornings were never an easy time, even with Skye constantly at her side, but as the day progressed she often found renewed energy, focus and courage that life would be good again one day, and things would pick up.

She was a one hundred percent sort of person, in whatever she attempted whether relationships, work, or in her role as a mother. She often took things too far, and took life too seriously. Cora was very much a Gemini and definitely knew how to have fun; that was one side of her. The other was the very sensible and responsible, dutiful woman, who liked things done in a certain way. She was, generally, a traditional individual, in an old-fashioned manner and she didn't give much lee-way. Patience was not her thing.

She knew that her serious side was not often displayed over her choice of men. She had tried to teach her children right from wrong, the one thing she had promised to do to her maximum abilities, and had done it well. And that mission hadn't stopped as they grew older. In fact she had never stopped keeping them on what she considered to be the right path, and a lot of her happiness in her adult life had come from Francis, Belle and Ludo.

She adored them and they meant everything to her.

She was immensely proud of them and had done a good job as a mother. As good as she could have done under the circumstances, or so she believed whole heartedly, although the circumstances could have been far better… had she not made such a shambles of her romantic liaisons.

Cora loved her work. She had always been interested in politics and wrote for a national tabloid on a weekly basis.

Her father had died quite young, at fifty-nine, and

unexpectedly of cancer, at the same time as Cora was going through a separation from her husband, Mark.

As a consequence this time in her life had become quite overwhelming. She had been hit by an avalanche of anxieties, mainly health-related, some of which she had managed to address with the help of a marvellous Irish counsellor, Linda, with whom she had been having therapy. She had been seeing Linda for nearly a year.

Seeing Linda had helped Cora enormously. Cora's anxiety had not significantly receded since then, but now she was much better at finding ways to cope with it.

She could go through many months of life's ups and downs, with her fears of ill-health sidelined by either periods of happiness, or worry about other issues, but it never quite left her alone.

Reflecting on her life now, she could see how her fear of dying, or becoming terminally ill, was troubling her, perhaps particularly as her father had passed away at a comparatively young age.

Cora was only too aware that her anxieties had made their way into the relationships she had enjoyed in the past twenty years since leaving her husband. This had not only been a cause of negative consequences, but at times, catastrophic ones. But, she was very good at hiding the truth, and of course, there were many other reasons why things hadn't always worked out.

After splitting up from her latest partner, Sebastian, Cora's relationship with her ex-husband, Mark, had hit a terrible low. She had found it very hard to relate to him at all, so they had only met up on special occasions that involved the boys and Belle. Things were better between them now.

The fact that her relationship with Sebastian hadn't worked out had given Mark a lot of ammunition to be resentful and bitter towards her, at a time when she could have really done with his support. Since their divorce, they had enjoyed a reasonably amicable and honest frienship, which had certainly been a blessing for the children. But Mark had, on more than one occasion, accused her of unsettling Francis, Belle and Ludo, especially when they were younger, because of her choices of companions.

Cora had always been a carer at heart and this sentiment had thoroughly influenced her choice of men, men that she had the habit of rescuing…

She tended to be organised and efficient, and gave the impression of having a controlled power. She was a 'sorter', a 'saviour' but she was aware that this had been her downfall.

Cora's companions, had been, on the whole, intelligent and entertaining men, the souls of a party, but emotionally hopelessly immature. And often too passionate and impulsive which had brought with it financial problems as well.

She had been intensely in love more than once in her life but only once had she encountered the kind of love that buries itself so extraordinarily deep within every bone of your body, that the feeling of it, is also able to cause so much pain.

Her lover, Stefano, a charming Argentinean man who had been living and working in London for nearly twenty years, was an incredibly passionate and romantic man, and their liaison had been, Cora could never forget, the stuff of dreams.

He had, from the start of their relationship and on many occasions later, been hopeful that he could leave his wife, but had ultimately found a break from his family too traumatic.

Cora now knew, that she would never put herself or anyone else through that experience again. It had been the most significant relationship of her life on many levels and one she would never regret having, but, by far, the most unhealthy.

Magical moments spent together in hiding made for the most exciting times; the highs were beyond words, but the lows which followed each rendezvous, were more than she could ever cope with again. She remembered crying so much that she wondered now how it could have lasted so long.

Is the yearning and longing for what is not ours and what we cannot have, or at least cannot have straightforwardly, the one feeling which unleashes the strongest and most passionate of loves?

Cora had hated the fact of betraying someone's wife, had begged Stefano to end it, either with her or his marriage but he had been too weak and too in love. They both had.

They occasionally sent messages to each other still years later, knowing even if without saying it, that nothing had really changed. Love of that kind is so deeply rooted in your heart that nothing on earth can ever replace or delete it.

And Cora had eventually moved on and had had two additional long relationships since, where she was conscious that falling in love in that same utterly intense way was not an option. Love was there, but of a very different kind. She had pursued relationships that she judged to be stable and safe and good for her.

Mainly good for her.

At least the men were single and available but sadly these relationships had failed too.

As Cora tended to choose needy men, it seemed to take her

two or three years to realise that no man can truly be rescued and she would then be surprised and fed up that none of them seem to pick themselves up and be the person she had imagined they would become, when 'mended', and were not in the least interested in listening to her concerns.

She had done this, three times and, for some inexplicable reason, she had been unable to stop this pattern from happening again. None of Cora's past companions had been any good at helping her through her anxieties and worries, because of their own hidden ones. This grew as time went by, when most of her emotional energy was exhausted by looking after them and their families. This was especially true when young children were also involved, whom she always treated as her own.

When she walked away from her relationships, she tended to feel huge amounts of short-lived relief. She would 'nest' herself back in her cottage, making everything cosy and beautifully ready for her children's next visit. It was as if a celebration of a new start was about to take place, and Cora would pour all her love on Francis, Belle and Ludo and lose herself in being their mother. At times in a nearly stifling way, especially when the boys were in their late teens, or early twenties, and didn't necessarily feel like being constantly hugged and kissed!

Belle was the closest one in character to Cora and would never say no to an overabundance of affection.

But Cora was realistic and knew that life alone was not what she ultimately wanted, neither was it good for her. Solitude allowed her to ponder too much on herself and her apprehensions, so companionship was by far the better outcome. Her sister Laura had encouraged her to spend at least a year alone and she was coming up for that.

Laura always seemed to have a sensible answer to everything. She was as practical as Cora was dreamy; viewed Cora as unrealistic and at times, accused her of verging on the dramatic. All attributes that she believed were acceptable in your teens but not in your twenties, let alone your thirties and forties and most definitely, completely ridiculous in your fifties.

Laura had married well; Colin was a stockbroker and, although pretty dull, had been a good husband to her and they had, what seemed, a good life. But then Laura had never been the sort of woman who had high expectations of men or their affections. She was tough and independent and although she wanted Colin to be a good provider, she enjoyed a very comfortable life making the most of what they had, and she never seemed to moan about her marriage or life in general. Cora didn't necessarily believe that this meant that her sister was deeply happy at all but just that she had a different view of happiness from her own. Their children seemed to have matured into practical and stable individuals like their parents, and all had good jobs in London. Cora had of course often felt jealous of their steady lifestyle. She used to make herself feel better by imagining waking up next to Colin every morning and thinking herself lucky that, on most days, she would open her eyes to stare down the bed at her lovely Labrador, Skye, instead!

2

This particular weekend, she had written down two things she was determined to do in the next few days, and knew she had to stick to it.

The first was to get in touch with her well-meaning, but rather nosy neighbour, Jill. She had been very supportive of her through the last year and, a good ear when Cora seemed to have run out of people to go to.

Jill certainly wasn't her first choice of friends, which may sound harsh, but she was the one who had really pushed the relationship into fith gear, as soon as she could, and thought of little more than to find Cora the perfect life companion.

Jill was constantly suggesting mature, steady and financially secure men. 'He is just the job for you Cora,' she would say.

Cora was yet to come across anyone she had suggested that she would award a five out of ten. But it was time to be polite and accept her dinner invitation for this coming Saturday, as Jill had left three messages on her voicemail already and Cora couldn't quite face another one.

The second was to go and see her mother, Belinda, who recently, had not been well. Cora kept visits to her mother few and far between, unless absolutely necessary, which included the 'must days' like birthdays and Christmas; Belinda Patterson had always spoken her mind, and as she got older, even more so. This often came as something that Cora didn't appreciate as, like her sister Laura, Belinda was of a very practical, no-nonsense disposition. Love and passion were things that belong in films and her view of most things was… 'you just have to get on with it, girl'… not Cora's view on life.

Belinda had retired to a small, but attractive house in a village about twenty-five miles away. This was a perfect distance, near enough, in case of emergencies, but not close enough for her to be popping in to her eldest daughter for casual cups of coffee.

The house had been beautifully designed by an architect who had been a colleague of her father's. It had large windows facing south which let in huge waves of light through the day, cleverly reflected on the beautiful, contemporary mirrors hanging in the open plan kitchen. Mirrors which Cora had always admired greatly, but nevertheless had also worried that they might reflect the sunlight and set the house on fire. Her mother considered this to be old nonsense.

Belinda was good at decorating and had a way of making everything look cosy and welcoming, but at the same time utterly uncluttered and rather grand, even for a reasonably small house. She had mixed old with new in a way that worked, where it so often doesn't, and Cora admired this in her… one of the few things she did admire of her mother nowadays.

They hadn't always had a strained relationship, in fact Cora remembered a fairly happy childhood. But when her marriage to Mark had broken down, while the children were still young, her mother had seemed to have lost her tolerance and acceptance towards Cora.

After their divorce, Belinda found it increasingly hard to show much support towards her daughter, and Cora hadn't forgotten it.

She had tried to make some sense of it, as she had been desperate not to lose her mother's affection, through a time where life was already such a struggle.

She had failed to see a path through it and their relationship had stagnated, turning into what was now a polite, brief and at times monosyllabic exchange of family news.

So she only visited Belinda rarely.

Cora caught her reflection on the hall mirror as she went to open the door to Skye who had been lying quietly on the door mat outside. She closed the front door and, with Saturday evening's dinner party on her mind, she stopped in front of the mirror. She thought hard about something nice to say about herself.

She tried to imagine herself from another person's point of view, as if waiting for a verdict. Well, she hadn't made any effort today, but then she wasn't expecting to see anyone. What was staring back at her wasn't impressive, she had to admit. In fact, a little frightening.

Cora was the sort of person who never wore make up, or nice clothes, unless she was going out. She just didn't see the point and felt most comfortable in a pair of leggings or loose trousers, with a big jumper to cover her hips, which she had always considered to be out of proportion for her tall frame.

Cora could transform herself from looking below average to very smart in a short time with a little effort. And, on the whole, she enjoyed the results. She felt a certain amount of pride in that. Even though, she had put on three quarters of a stone in the last year, she could still get away with it. After all, many of her friends looked far worse, she thought, in a flash of child-like wickedness… fatter, but probably far happier, was the immediate afterthought, as they no doubt had someone who loved them dearly. Whatever their shape and size.

She had recently started looking at her wrinkles with more attention, wondering whether they now regularly appeared overnight.

'Is this what happens to everyone after they reach 50?' she asked herself… She had never particularly worried about them before.

She regrouped, pushing away any thoughts of comparisons with others which would only lower her morale further. The telephone rang and she checked the number before answering, only to see that it was Jill. Perfect nuisance but perfect nevertheless, as it saved her making the call later.

As Cora accepted the invitation for Saturday, Jill sounded unusually excited, and announced that her brother was coming from Ireland, and would be bringing a friend, before going to watch cricket at the Oval.

She had invited the Brownes, from the Old Rectory, whom Cora had yet to meet, and two girlfriends from her book club, one of whom had recently been widowed.

Cora's first thought was, 'poor girl, her husband has just died, and Jill is already trying to find her a new one.' Little did she know that the only person Jill was truly hoping to lead to cupid, was Cora herself.

Jill was in her mid-sixties, and most of her friends were either the same age or older. Jill's husband, who had left her many years before for a younger version, would now be in his mid-seventies. Cora took a deep sigh, and thought, 'it will be good for me to get out of the house and meet new people.' She really had hardly made any effort at all since leaving Sebastian, and it was now nearly a year.

She promised herself to push the boat out this week-end, however damp the sand felt under her feet. She needed to get past those first waves of self-doubt and deep anxieties, those driven by her nature, and others probably driven by the ups and downs of the menopause.

She would do her best, both on the looks front and in terms of mood. Cora would try not to view the dinner party as she always used to…

She would attend with the view that it would be a night out rich in conversations, with new and interesting people. That was good enough. It would be a first step towards normality. Getting out there again and not living under a shadow.

She would wear something pretty, high heels, (her shoes had always been her friends), and good heels would make her legs look longer and give her more confidence. It was extraordinary how shoes, far more than a dress, could make her feel rather sexy and raise her self-esteem. This was why, when she prepared for an evening out, Cora would nearly always start this task from choosing her shoes before her clothes.

She had a large collection of shoes, and every single pair had meant something important to her.

Not necessarily a happy memory, but a memory nonetheless. She would choose carefully as she didn't wish to look too obviously single and available, but attractive enough to get noticed and spark a little interest.

Subtle.

Even if none of the men were her type at all. She would see it as a test; a test of her confidence and to get her back into the swing of things.

Cora called her mother and abruptly, all silly thoughts of clothes and shoes and flirty nights out, came to a halt.

Belinda's stern tone on the phone, almost accusatory, reminded Cora of the child within her, and her anxiety and tension returned. 'How could this happen so quickly?' she thought with regret, 'how could a joyous moment be followed so rapidly by sorrow in this way.'

She tried to arrange to go for tea the next day, but her mother didn't seem keen.

'Why don't we try week after next Cora, I have a lot on. Thank you but I am fine, you don't need to visit me to check that I am fine. You can just ring me.'

Cora felt as if she had just been scolded like you would a young child and tried to force any thought of her mother to the back of her mind.

Laura, her sister, would no doubt say, 'You haven't tried hard enough, you should just turn up, and make sure she is fine.'

Cora knew this attitude was partly due to her sister's feeling of guilt. Laura knew that, having Cora living close to their mother, was a huge advantage.

Time to go for a speedy walk with Skye who had never let her down and gave her unconditional love at all times. Even if her breath was a bit smelly nowadays! Walks are the best medicine of all, thought Cora. It was raining but this would only serve to making her feel better about being out of the house and in the fresh air.

Saturday came quickly and suddenly Cora realised, that maybe she didn't feel quite as brave as she had initially expected about facing a new crowd, let alone feeling flirty and dressing up.

She rang Carol, her very close friend, hoping to get some

encouragement and a bit of reassurance.

Carol lived in London and had known Cora since they had sat opposite each other, in their first job after leaving university, as journalists for a local newspaper. She had Skye's sister, Bumble, a beautiful pale yellow Labrador, and lived in a small terraced house in Battersea, which had belonged to her parents. She had never married or had children, but had five godchildren whom she adored and spoiled rotten.

Carol had a pretty, angular face, with striking thick auburn curly hair and a big voice, which she was often teased about. She was slightly untidy and bohemian in her appearance and often wore long, colourful tunics to hide her large figure.

She was a size eight shoe, and a heart the size of her feet. Cora had never met a kinder person.

She had graduated from Oxford University and had gone on to study for two further years in America, living in Washington, which had given her a very good understanding of American politics.

Cora had also tried to contact Kitty, another of 'the team', hoping to share her thoughts about the evening ahead, but Kitty was on her annual family holiday in France. Cora didn't feel she could disturb her over something quite so silly.

Kitty also lived in London and had not only been to school with Cora, but also shared a flat with her at University, so they knew each other very well. She was quite petite and, unlike Carol, only a size three shoe! Everything about Kitty was neat and organised. She was pretty, in a very wholesome, and English way. She had very light blonde thick hair, which she had worn both short and long since her childhood, and she was one of those people fortunate enough to suit most styles, because her facial features were very good.

She had fabulous cheek bones and a small nose and pale skin with a few freckles and could easily get away with only wearing a little mascara and some lip gloss, rather than having to worry about her complexion and needing to cover it in foundation and powder. She always looked good, even first thing in the morning after a late night, which had been a long-standing joke, between her and Cora.

She worked as a wealth manager in the City and had had a brilliant career, for someone who had managed to produce five children. She had also taken care of a rather financially hopeless but very endearing man, Victor. He had been the house husband who had, after all, made Kitty's dream possible.

He was both rather overweight, and overly clumsy, but had made a loyal and steady companion to a very ambitious and driven woman, whose focus had been to succeed in as many areas of her life as possible. Cora called her 'Superwoman'.

Cora had often regretted not pursuing a better, more ambitions path after University, building a good career for herself which would with no doubt have given her far more self-confidence. Instead she had been attracted to the sort of men who promised an easier and more comfortable life.

Writing for the paper, had provided a regular income, albeit a small one, but Cora viewed it more like a hobby than a job.

She loved it so much.

She was very aware that she could have done better for herself had she tried harder, but she had married early and had relied on Mark, once the children had arrived, to keep them afloat financially, while the paper had merely boosted their life-style.

When she and Mark had divorced, she had been able to buy her cottage out of the divorce settlement so she was lucky enough to be mortgage-free.

Cora had told Carol about Jill's dinner party only a couple of days before and her dear friend had been very excited for her, making up all sorts of funny scenarios. It made Cora laugh out loud, and they both giggled like teenagers. Although that had been fun, when the conversation had ended, Cora found herself sitting alone in the house reflecting on what they had discussed. She soon realised that all she was causing by sharing this information, was to raise expectations, both in her own mind and that of her dearest friend. Raising expectations to levels that were bound to come crashing down by Sunday morning, and she knew she couldn't afford that yet…

Cora had spent the last year getting mentally and physically stronger after her breakup from Sebastian; she had promised herself that no man, would ever cause her to feel so low and so bad about herself again.

She had poured every inch of her skin, every drop of her blood, into her relationship with him, only to find that he wasn't in love with her or at least, not as much as she had believed. Not enough to hold their relationship together… to glue it back when it came unstuck so many times.

And the worst part of it was that he was quite happy to carry on as they were. Sebastian kept telling her that they were just like many other couples and would say, 'when love and passion dies down Cora, you should know, one is left with fondness and tolerance.'

Thinking back at his words, made Cora still feel so devastated that after only three years together this had been his view of their relationship. She had fought hard to get it back to a much happier level, believing she truly could, as she was an eternal hoper but at the end, she had abandoned her heroic efforts, after realising he was making none himself.

Just as she was reminiscing about unhappy times with Sebastian, the phone rang, and she didn't recognise the number. She was tempted not to reply as Skye was staring at her with wanton eyes, but in the last few years, Cora felt a little nervous that any missed call may be the one that alerted her that something had happened to her mother so, heavy-heartedly, she answered.

Cora hadn't been too far off the mark.

It wasn't with regards to her mother though. It was about Jill.

Helena Browne introduced herself to Cora and told her that she had been walking her dog across the village green an hour before and had seen an ambulance leaving the short drive to Jill's house. An ambulance in a small village always caught people's attentive eyes… and tongues.

She had rung Jill and got no answer so had returned home, called a friend who had a daughter who was a nurse at Peplow Hospital, where she suspected she may have been taken, and she had managed to find out that Jill had broken her leg.

Jill had then called her, a few minutes later, from her mobile, to explain the eventful afternoon at home. She had asked Helena to get in touch with all the invitees for tonight, begging them to come anyway as the table was laid, wine was waiting, and food would be ready. Jenny, her part-time housekeeper, had been booked to come and help.

'It would be mad not to take advantage of everything and let it all go to waste', Jill had told Helena, especially as Jill's brother, Rupert, was going to be staying anyway with his friend and, it would be far more fun for them to meet some of the locals.

Cora had to smile to herself, and while listening to Helena describing the events with a mixture of drama and not a little surprise, she suddenly realised the evening was taking a rather curious turn.

She put herself in the same position, and thought that she would never wish to have people coming into her house, her safe nest, to attend her own dinner party, while she was lying in a hospital having her leg operated on!

She admired Jill enormously for her courage and, in some ways, for her ability to detach herself from the sentimental lock Cora felt over her own belongings.

'I wish I was more like her' mumbled Cora to herself while Helena was still on the other line. But that was never going to be her…

Her insecurities would see to that.

Why had Cora found it so hard to push aside her lack of confidence, one which still held her back from moving on and being able to embrace the intrusive eyes of near strangers around spaces she considered to be so deeply part of her and her alone?

Her mind wondered briefly over what she felt were those spaces and a smile immediately formed on her lips. Because those spaces were her home, her cottage, her beloved things and all her memories, and they made her feel secure.

And they meant more to her than she could ever start to explain, even to a dear friend.

Cora viewed some of her furniture like one would a person.

She had often felt that this attachment to things was possibly replacing the attachment she had formed in her past relationships for her partners and, subsequently lost.

So there was something extra special about the feeling of safety of holding on to the memories from an old piece of furniture, which you know is going to welcome you home every day, and belongings, unlike people, did not judge, or condemn. Only offered unconditional love. Like Skye.

Cora had moved in three times, with different partners, over the past twenty years and, on each occasion, made wherever they lived together, into a lovely cosy home.

She was generous, kind and very sensitive to the feelings children often have when two families merge together.

Cora always tried to have a fair mix of furniture, pictures and photographs in the house so that everyone living there, even if not all the time, felt that they were surrounded by something familiar.

But there was nothing quite like sitting on your own old and frayed comfy sofa, surrounded by the warmth that can only really be generated by things that have a deep and emotional meaning to you.

And she had experienced that feeling of 'coming home' quite a few times now.

And although Cora didn't enjoy being alone and didn't wish to grow old alone, she remained quite fearful of going wrong again, and going through that very process of house moving once more.

The bringing together of families, which Cora had experienced three times now and, the injecting of a huge amount of emotional energy into that process as nothing she did was ever half hearted, had taken its toll on her.

Cora knew that tonight she must keep her sensible side wide awake and just enjoy the evening for what it was. 'No expectations' she repeated to herself… 'none whatsoever'.

'I must be strong' she thought out loud. 'Strong and not foolish.'

If she had managed a year without the love of a man, she could surely go further, until she felt absolutely sure, she was not making another mistake.

But what Cora couldn't possibly have imagined, was that the consequences of that evening's dinner party were in fact about to change her life for ever.

And in more ways than one…

3

As Cora opened her wardrobe to start filtering through her many clothes, the telephone rang again. This was turning out to be one of her busiest afternoons for a long time. She would often be in the house alone and would not speak to anyone at all for as long as two or three days apart from the occasional chat to Alan, the lovely postman.

Alan was a delightful man and had at times hovered on the doorstep when he noticed Cora was just in the kitchen, hoping to catch her before she went for a walk with Skye. He enjoyed their brief encounters, because he genuinely cared and wanted to make sure she was ok. He knew she lived alone and was hardly ever away nowadays. Cora worried that he might be lonely. Alan Parson's wife had passed away a couple of years before, and he was finding loneliness very painful. But while Cora struggled a little in the mornings but found courage and strength as the day went on, Alan was the opposite. His shift started very early but he would be back home by 3pm at the latest and having smiled and chatted to many people till then, he now found walking into the emptiness of his cottage quite frightening so he would go about switching the radio and the television on, so as not be engulfed in the silence of his own slow movements and breaths.

Cora's call was from Jill. She had been booked in to have surgery the next morning, but they were keeping her at the hospital till then, as her leg had swollen up so much that they preferred to keep her monitored. She sounded in remarkably good spirits and kept saying what a fool she felt for having fallen down the stairs at her age. She asked Cora to play hostess, as she doubted her brother Rupert would do a very good job of it after a couple of drinks, and she also knew Cora would look after everyone.

'Goodness…' thought Cora.

The dynamics of the evening were changing again and this time not in a way she welcomed. From a simple invitation that she had felt unsure whether to accept, she had now been asked to host a dinner party in someone else's house, with complete strangers. This, she felt, required a far larger slice of self-confidence than she had anticipated.

She slumped in the pretty blue armchair that had been her grandmother's, the one person she could give anything to still have with her now. She felt all her courage run out of her, flowing away from her head down to her toes and out in an estuary where it would not be recovered. Cora closed her eyes wondering whether she could just call the whole evening off and get into her bed and pretend today had been a mistake.

Maybe she had just imagined the whole thing, and could wake tomorrow and carry on with her rather insular but safe life. She felt hot and told herself she must not panic and let that little voice inside her get the better of her. She was going to not only show up, but look amazing and make Jill proud. She had to. She must.

She wondered whether she might have time for a half an hour snooze; that would make her feel much better… and before she could answer that question, Cora had nodded off.

By the time she awoke, she realised she had less than an hour to shower, wash and straighten her unruly, wild hair, before making her way to Jill's, ideally before the other guests. She should at least meet Rupert first, as she was supposedly hosting the dinner with him. She started to wonder what he might be like…

Cora's choice of what to wear, came to her quickly, not because she had planned it at all, but because of the lack of time. She wore a black satin knee-length skirt, which was very forgiving to her thighs, as it had just enough give in it from years of wear, to make it feel very comfortable; a black sleeveless top and a long, bright red, floaty cardigan. She selected a pair of red shoes, real old friends, but still looked in very good shape, pointed with high heels. She remembered buying them at least six years before at a sale in L K Bennett on the King's Road. She had been so excited about them, that she could only bare to look at them for the first three months, as if they were a 'hard won' trophy, before plucking up the courage to wear them. Cora adored shoe shopping, although she hadn't done any for some time now.

She rushed downstairs, fed and rushed the dog into the garden, called her back in after only a few minutes, kissed her warmly on the head, and looked at herself in the hall mirror. She had done a remarkably good job, in what had scarcely been half- an- hour. Her hair had not been her main enemy today as on most days and looked pretty. The red cardigan, resting on the black skirt, with its straight unfussy lines and no patterns, somehow created an air of decisiveness and self-confidence.

Good result, thought Cora, congratulating herself although of course the appearance hardly reflected how she really felt inside, but she had succeeded in creating a very good mask behind which she could hide, at least for the next few hours.

As Cora walked down her short drive and turned towards Jill's house, she caught a glimpse of an old E-type Jaguar driving towards her. It was black and reflecting the evening sun on its polished surface. There was something strangely familiar about it…

Cora had always loved classic cars, and recognised many of the makes from a long way off.

As the car approached towards her, she noticed that it was one of the very early ones, from the sixties, and stared in admiration. But as the Jaguar took a sharp turn up Jill's drive, Cora, quickly turned her face away, aware that she had been caught staring at it like a child.

She wasn't going to arrive at the house before the other guests after all, as well as looking more than silly, peering at some of them on their way to dinner!

Not exactly the start she had hoped for.

'Well' she said to herself, 'it can only get better'…

She reached for the handle on Jill's heavy front door just as it opened. A huge smile reached her before she even had the time to take in the face behind it. Her immediate thought was that it must be Rupert.

'How do you do, I am Raith Browne,' he said as he stretched out his hand.

Cora noticed long elegant fingers and a well-worn signet ring.

Raith was tall and definitely handsome and probably in his late sixties or early seventies. Cora could tell he was a charmer before anything more had really been said. She had come across enough characters like him and wasn't going to be drawn in by the openly flirtatious type.

Then she immediately remembered Helena's conversation earlier in the day. Raith was of course, her husband, too old for Cora anyway and therefore any flirting would be no doubt just out of habit and to make her feel at ease.

She must stop analysing men, after having just shaken their hand, and try and relax and enjoy tonight. Had Jill told everyone about her having been single for some time, and a little nervous…?

Cora sincerely hoped not.

In the kitchen, she saw Jill's lovely housekeeper, Jenny, who seemed to have everything under control.

'Go and relax Cora and meet the other guests' she said, 'I will bring some canapés through in a few moments.'

Did Jenny know everything about her life too?

She realised that it would not be unrealistic to believe that the whole village would be likely to be aware of her circumstances, her romantic mishaps, the difficult relationships she had with her mother, her near perfect sister Laura, and long suffering ex-husband, Mark.

This made Cora feel even more nervous.

She had planned to keep herself busy, helping Jen in the kitchen through the evening, which would have given her something useful to do, and also, the excuse to be able to move around, without getting stuck in conversation with anyone.

Sadly, now, that seemed unlikely to happen.

By about eight fifteen in the evening all the guests had arrived, and, to Cora's relief, they all seemed friendly. She felt herself relax a little.

Helena, Raith's wife, seemed a little tense. Cora hoped this might take the attention off her own nervousness, although she knew, this was not a particularly kind thing to wish for.

Never having met her before, Cora couldn't be sure whether, this was part of her everyday characteristic or, whether she was upset about something, but she wasn't going to make it her mission to find out either way tonight.

This evening was about her, her first steps back into normal living and socialising, and hopefully having a little fun. Tonight, she was going to be a little selfish as Carol, her dear friend, had been telling her for years... 'you must learn to be selfish and stop always trying to save everyone.'

It was only half-way through the main course that Cora suddenly realised that Rupert's friend wasn't there.

Had she misheard Jill on the phone?

She recalled something about the cricket, and they must have been at the Oval, or Old Trafford that day, or the day before, and he must have changed his plan and returned home after it.

Cora congratulated herself on the fact that it had taken her a couple of hours to realise that one of the men who was meant to attend, wasn't there at all.

One of only three.

This was not the Cora of days gone by. She was succeeding in keeping her past expectations at bay and not viewing the evening as a guaranteed blind date, however much she had previously giggled about it over the phone with Carol...

She had heard so much about Rupert over the past few years.

This was not necessarily because Jill spoke about him with such regularity, but more due to the fact that Cora often felt the need to deviate their conversation away from her own life, and her many dramas, by showing a polite interest in him.

Jill, on the other hand, loved every minute that was spent talking about other people's misfortunes, and ever eventful circumstances; listening to Cora and trying to advise her since her own husband had left, was one of her favourite pastimes.

This had been especially true, since Jill's daughter Sally, and grandchildren had moved to France.

They had lived very close by, until their first grandchild had been born, and then decided to buy a farm near Limoges and start a new life there. Her son in law's family, the Traceys, had farmed nearby for four generations.

After Peter, Sally's husband, had inherited the land, they had earned a reasonable sum of money from the installation of six wind turbines, which had allowed them to further their horizons.

They had rented out their beautiful old farmhouse and the farm land, and had moved on, all within the space of six months.

With her grandmother's duties now limited to a handful of times a year, Jill had found herself full of free time to dedicate to her friends!

Rupert, who was on Cora's right, suddenly noticed that she seemed distracted by something or someone and felt he should come to her rescue, by noisily turning his chair by forty-five degrees until he was practically sitting on top of her!

'So, dear girl, tell me all about yourself. I want to know everything,' he said giggling loudly.

Cora was left with no choice but to stare straight into his eyes, feeling suddenly terribly shy and cornered. She took a sip of her wine, allowing her heartbeat to slow a little, before thinking of how to reply to him, without drawing the attention of the rest of the guests.

Rupert was charmingly, loud and boyish. Like a man who hasn't really matured enough emotionally and lacks the sensitivity that Cora knew was vital for her in a partner, if she was ever going to share her life with anyone again.

From first impressions, Cora believed Rupert was the kind of person who would suit a far more independent and stronger partner than herself. She guessed that he was the sort of man who didn't need to rely on the love of another, to feel completely happy, but enjoyed it, purely as a bonus to a relationship.

Cora of course was well- aware that to rely on another too much, was a sign of weakness. Possibly a downfall, as it opened the door to disappointments, but she had to stick to what was realistic. She knew why and where she had gone wrong in the past, and could only hope to have learned from her mistakes, without pretending she could ever change from the person she really felt deep down.

She just needed to be more cautious with her choices, if the time ever came to have to make choices again...

Cora was so absorbed in her own thoughts, possibly by having spent so much time alone over the past year, that she hadn't realised that Rupert was looking at her with a confused expression on his face.

'Caution?' he said. 'Caution over what my dear?' he repeated.

Cora realised she must have been thinking aloud.

This had been embarrassing, but it had kick started her into what was now a flowing chat about her cottage, village life and her dog, deviating the conversation from anything too personal, and allowing everyone around the table to join in as they wished.

Cora was doing well. She felt she was been perfectly charming and inclusive. Her own confidence had no doubt been boosted by finishing what was now her second glass of wine.

Jill would have been impressed and delighted that all her guests were getting on so well!

By the time pudding had been served, Rupert had had quite a lot to drink and was getting louder and louder and, although his jokes were entertaining, Cora wasn't sure this was going to turn into one of those memorable evenings where you return home at 3am.

Raith, who had chosen to sit opposite her but not beside her, to Cora's relief, had been interesting and perfectly polite, without the flirtatious side he seemed to have clearly demonstrated when they had first met by Jill's front door.

In fact, he seemed to be much more subdued than she expected him to be.

Cora suspected the reason for this may have been because of Helena's presence in the room.

Helena still seemed a little tense, and definitely not as comfortable as she had come across during their telephone conversation.

Cora thought back at the lovely Jaguar parked outside, and imagined Raith driving it round the countryside, with his beaming smile but couldn't quite place his wife in it beside him. It was just like when one first meets a couple, who to the naked and critical eye, seem totally unsuited to each other, and one starts guessing what might have brought them together in the first place.

Something about Raith's car, had reminded Cora of her childhood but she couldn't recall her parents ever having one.

They were far more practical than that. Somebody in their village must have had an E-type Jaguar, or was it similar to a car used in a television programme?

Cora had been keen on cars from an early age.

She often played a silly game as a child, whenever her parents used to drive her sister Laura and her to Cornwall for their holidays.

Hours were spent during the car journey, asking 'are we nearly there?' and 'we are hungry, when are we stopping?'

To help her pass the time, Cora would stare at all passing cars, making up stories about the passengers, and it would keep her, and the rest of the family, when allowed to share her imagination with them, entertained for hours. She remembers the best times were had when watching animated conversations between driver and passenger and, imaging some very dramatic goings on, wondering whether the couple in question would make up and kiss, or separate by consequence.

Not that separating or divorce were events that Cora had any real understanding about as a child.

All she knew, were the tales that her friend, Anna from school, used to tell her about her own time, split between her mother and father. The wonderful holidays she would have, as her divorced parents regularly competed against each other to give their children the most expensive and exotic trips round the world, and all accompanied by more presents she could ever imagine.

Anna's parents had obviously done a good job at making their separation into something rather adventurous for their children and, on the surface, seemingly, not in the least traumatic.

Cora was of course now old enough to understand that

all the material spoiling Anna had talked about, was hardly a healthy way of pretending your parents hadn't split up, but she remembers quite clearly thinking, at the time, that divorce sounded rather exciting. Thinking back to when she was young, Cora also realised that people then didn't discuss their private life quite so openly as they did nowadays. Social media didn't exist, so one was not so constantly aware of everybody's business and the daily changes within it.

So it wasn't so surprising that Cora had always had an extraordinary imagination, which is why she had been so dreamy about life in general rather than pragmatic and more realistic.

Probably the reason she was still on her own, Cora thought, opposed to her sister Laura who seemed to have everything worked out.

And Belinda, their mother, was so good at reminding her of her present circumstances…

Just when Cora was starting to wonder whether she had heard more than she necessarily wished about the village gossip from Jill's two book club friends, Anita and Lesley, she became aware of Jenny talking to someone by the front door.

Who could it be at this time?

Maybe Jill's daughter Sally had returned on the first flight from France to be with her mother in hospital, but after quick calculation, she realised that would be far-fetched, unless she had taken the journey in a missile, as the accident had only happened a few hours earlier.

Suddenly a man appeared; he looked rather coy but relieved.

4

Rupert literally jumped up from his seat to welcome his dear friend into the dining room. He made a space for him at the table and tapping his knife repeatedly on a glass, brought everyone's conversation to an immediate halt!

'Hear, hear,' he said rather too loudly, with his enthusiastic and thundering manner, one which Cora now recognised to be very much part of Rupert's rather overwhelming character.

'This is my very good friend Nicholas McDonald!'

Rupert carried on, to explain that Nicholas, had not been able to join them for dinner as initially hoped, but was in fact coming to stay for the night.

A glass of burgundy with a plate of cheese on which to nibble, was put in front of the new arrival and Cora, suddenly found she had been promoted to a seat beside Rupert's guest.

Cora was now on her third glass of wine and the sensible and cautious 'her' was slipping away fast, only to leave behind a very relaxed and chatty version of herself.

Nicholas looked rather adorable and innocent, and she decided he might be quite incapable of defending himself from the claws of this circle of carnivorous village elders, unless she tried to do something about it.

She wanted to help him and felt herself slipping into her full- on rescue mode. Cora had had a bit too much to drink by this point, for someone only used to a couple of glasses at the very most.

She hadn't been drinking for over three months and now saw the downside of that decision.

Just as she was starting to feel rather too warm, Jenny looked in the room briefly to say her goodnights, and they all thanked her so much for feeding them marvellously and, running everything so smoothly in her employer's absence.

Jenny had in fact owned a small event company until a couple of years before, so she was more than capable of running a small evening like this. She was a very special and humble person and was very grateful for the praise received.

Cora was looking at Nicholas wanting to place a label… a verdict on him, far too soon.

The wine was 'getting' to her.

She loved her wines and tonight's Gevrey Chambertin was such a treat.

She felt a little tipsy, recognising that she had been far more flirtatious that she would have the courage to be, while sober…or planned to be. Something about the man on her left, intrigued Cora, and Nicholas was looking at her with interest too.

The Irish gentleman was tall, with blonde hair and very strong cheek bones, which reminded Cora of some of the characters she had seen on television lately in a Scandinavian thriller. He wasn't what you would necessarily describe as strikingly good looking, but there was something hugely warm and attractive about him. He had very light blue, kind eyes.

Belinda always used to say to her… 'never trust a man with green eyes,' so she giggled to herself thinking she would have her mother's blessing with Nicholas.

But that, of course, would hardly be the case.

Belinda had looked at all Cora's past companions with great suspicion, and had never really warmed enough to any of them, not enough anyway for Cora to genuinely believe that her mother actually approved.

Even when Cora and Mark had announced their engagement, her mother hadn't been exactly overjoyed which had surprised them both, as Mark's parents had been close friends of the family for years.

By now Cora had concluded, that her very difficult mother could not bring herself to be truly happy for anyone else, so she must not wait for approvals or blessings, but just get on with her life and keep it as private as possible.

It was sad to feel this way, but it was Cora's line of defence.

Her thoughts tumbled back to Nicholas… she imagined him to be a sensible and responsible chap. Not in a matter of fact way but through sensitive and careful judgement… so why was such a seemingly nice person, still not married?

Nicholas looked in his mid-fifties but she didn't know anything about his career, or his family, and he may well have had ten children with four different women for all she knew.

She smiled at herself just because she was allowing her mind to wonder.

Cora thought this was good news, surely meaning that she was truly relaxing and starting to enjoy the evening, and maybe she shouldn't be so anxious about making another mistake at this early stage. How silly of her to worry; after all she was just making things up in her head, in an innocent way, that could bring no harm to anyone, least of all her.

Cora's habit in the past had been to allow herself to let go of her better judgement, let things just happen far too quickly, even while her sensible side was saying 'be careful' and, ultimately, what had made her slip into situations which were hardly ideal, were thoughts of her father.

He had been so young when he had died and had seemed desperately unhappy in those last few years of marriage to her mother, although he would never say a word against her.

Cora didn't wish for herself to end her life in the same way, in fact it was what she feared the most.

The fear that life may be cut short without the knowledge of having lived every day as happy as one could possibly be.

Tonight all those thoughts came rushing back, and those promises she used to make to herself after her father's death… Tonight, Cora didn't feel that sense of drowning in a sea of worries and anxieties, especially ones of getting cancer, as she so often did.

She was just a woman who was truly enjoying the moment.

The company was good too; the dinner party suddenly seemed to be coming together, although Jill's two book club friends had now left.

Or was it because they had left?

Anita Wellson and her sister in law, Lesley, had been nice enough but Cora had felt neither of them had shown any particular interest in her, Rupert's stories about his past adventures in Africa or, listening to Helena. Instead they had been far more focused on the drama surrounding Jill's accident, and what may or may not happen, during, and after the operation to mend her broken leg.

Cora unkindly thought that Jill's leg must have been the

most exciting thing in their rather dull life, and they were going to make the most of it.

Raith had convinced everyone to move from their original places at the dinner table, so to leave no gaps, and Cora found herself now in between Helena and Nicholas. Rupert had moved to the other side of the table.

As Raith had been the instigator of this move, which hadn't been completely necessary, as only two guests had left, one whom, in fact, had been sitting at the top of the table, Cora remained intrigued as to why he hadn't planned to end up sitting next to her.

Cora's thoughts remained on Raith for another moment, and again to the flirtatious manner he had welcomed her into Jill's house, while something in his attitude towards her during dinner, had definitely changed.

It had been a beautiful clear evening and quite light outside till about half an hour before.

Jill had chosen new curtains for her dining room and they did look fantastic… Cora now felt guilty not having made more of it, when Jill had asked her opinion last year.

She had been too caught up in her own circumstances, too concerned about herself to be able to take in the little joys of others, and share moments of happiness that were not necessarily born out of her own life… oh, that made her sound rather like Belinda… but then she was her daughter after all.

Horror, thought Cora, was she turning into her mother without realising? In many ways, Cora felt more comfortable now that they were left in candlelight, which seemed much softer and kinder. This is always true, unless of course, one is sitting far too close to a candlestick in which case, it could go either way.

She started to feel her skin warming up again and hoped nobody would notice. Cora kept her fingers crossed that this was due to a quick hot flush which would come and go, and not the result of too much wine, in which case she may already be looking like Bridget Jones arriving at the lawyers annual Ball!

She would excuse herself and go and check. She suddenly remembered that she had forgotten to put her small make up pouch into her evening bag, while swapping things over from her old and very well used navy 'Longchamp', so she may have to slip upstairs into Jill's bathroom, and borrow some powder or foundation, if things were not looking good.

She hadn't anticipated drinking a bit too much, neither had she imagined to still be worrying about wanting to look her best well into the late evening, but she was sitting next to a lovely man and wanted to get to know him a little better.

Jill's bedroom had large bay windows, and was done up in a cool blue, which Cora felt was rather more masculine than she would have liked for her own room.

Jill had had the room painted that colour after her husband had left her. The curtains and the bedcover matched, and both had stripes on them. The window seats were of a darker shade of blue. Nothing in fact was particularly feminine about it; no flowers in a vase, candles and soft shades.

Only two photographs adorned Jill's bedroom, both strangely enough of Jill as a child, playing with a dog in front of a large house which must have been her parent's home.

Cora had only been upstairs once before, and hadn't really taken in the fact that the room seemed to her as if it was stripped of anything remotely to do with a woman's presence in it.

She couldn't be sure whether the décor was meant to be a reminder of Jill's husband or, a reflection of how Jill felt about herself since he had gone.

To reach the bathroom, Cora had had to walk past Jill's bedroom first, then her dressing room, and while passing through, her eyes had fallen on a leather weekend bag; it had been dropped by the side of the dressing table and it lay open with a shirt and a pair of men's trousers casually overflowing over the opened zip.

It seemed a little odd that Rupert may be sleeping in Jill's bedroom tonight, as the house had plenty of other rooms. He had maybe chosen to change there as the bathroom was next door. Quickly, remembering what her mission upstairs had been all about, Cora fastened her step and headed towards the bathroom, to try and do her best with what was left of her evening.

On her return downstairs, Cora found everyone had left the dining room. Had she been that long? Had her exit from the room acted as a sign that the evening should probably be over and had made Raith and Helena feel it was time to go, releasing her of her duty as hostess?

She walked into the drawing room slightly surprised that the Brownes had indeed left without saying goodbye, only to find Rupert and Nicholas, comfortably sitting on a large red sofa, with a whisky each. She was unsure of what her next move should be, as this might have easily been her sign that the evening was over, and about time she left the old friends to catch up with each other, but just as she looked around for her shawl, they both stood up and invited her to squeeze in between them.

The conversations that took place between the three of them, over the next two and a half hours, seemed to flow like between the oldest of friends. Cora learned that Raith and Helena's marriage had been on the rocks for a long time, and that they had bought the Rectory in the village to try and turn things around, after what they suspected was probably an affair. They had three children, and a number of grandchildren, some of whom lived reasonably close to their previous home, so it must have been a very brave decision to leave them behind in Shropshire and come as far as Hampshire.

Raith had been in the army and had spent a lot of time away from home over the years, with some of that serving abroad. He had always had a passion for classic cars but had recently sold his small collection, apparently to only retain his one absolute favourite, the Jaguar they had driven that evening. He had been posted in Hampshire at the start of his career and they both hoped that, living closer to some of their oldest friends, would bring back happier times for them both. At least that was the story that was circulating around the village. Rupert had learned all this news from Lesley, who had been sitting on his right at dinner.

By the end of the evening, the three of them were getting on so well, that they decided to meet up on Sunday for a pub lunch in the next-door village, after visiting Jill in hospital. Cora was walked home by Rupert which was a little disappointing, but she supposed it made sense, as he knew the way and was the only true host after all and, when he kissed her good bye on both cheeks, he laughed, and said, 'you made quite a hit on Nicholas, just as Jill thought you would.'

Cora didn't comment and just wanted to get into her bed now, with the memory of an unexpected lovely evening behind her.

And it had been a really great night.

Nicholas seemed extremely friendly, without being openly flirty, which made it even nicer somehow and his attention towards her, seemed very genuine.

What had Rupert meant?

Had Cora been too openly flirtatious with Nicholas after a little too much wine, followed by a glass of port.

She hoped not embarrassingly so.

She slipped into bed and surprised herself by not contemplating about how nice it may have been not to be alone now, but with Nicholas instead, which would have followed very much her old thought pattern.

Tonight, she just looked forward enormously to meeting him again the next day.

Something was different about Nicholas compared to 'the majority' of men she tended to fall for, but she wasn't quite sure what it was. The fact that he had not been flirtatious, but had engaged in charming and very attentive conversation, was certainly very attractive. She had felt comfortable chatting to him; cosy even, but not in a boring way at all, just safe in his company.

Nicholas had felt like the sort of person who would look after you if you were ill and would hold you in his arms if you were upset.

The fact that she couldn't tell whether he was interested in her physically or, as a potential girlfriend, didn't seem to matter to her at this point.

Not yet anyway, which was strange as Cora had so often relied on the sort of man who makes it very clear that he fancies you from very early on. And that, had suited her character.

What she couldn't be altogether sure of, was how much of this different sort of feeling, was born out of her own attitude towards him, caused by her past experiences, or the need that Cora felt to draw boundaries around her.

Nicholas was such a lovely man that he was bringing out a new side of her.

One thing Cora could be sure about was that she was allowing her imagination to play tricks on her tired and tipsy mind.

She was overthinking it and she knew that, what she really needed now, was a good sleep.

But just as her head had found a comfy place on her new down pillow and she had closed her eyes, her mobile beeped. Who could be sending her a message at this time of the night?

She then had a moment of panic thinking it may be one of the children, or news that her mother had suddenly been taken ill. They would have called her surely rather than texting, but then she had been out all evening.

Cora didn't recognise the number as one of her contacts which made her concerns increase; she started reading the first line of the message, but her eyes went straight to the end and it was signed by Raith.

This was very strange especially after his manner earlier on. If he was making a pass at her, this was certainly an unusual way to go about it, and he was quite a bit older than her.

But the message wasn't very long at all, and Raith seemed to be asking Cora to meet him next week sometime, possibly for a walk in the park, on the outskirts of Mollington, with their respective dogs.

He obviously can't have included Helena in this invitation, but neither, did he seem to be asking her to meet him somewhere particularly private.

Cora was left confused.

She didn't know what to think of it at all and she suddenly felt exhausted…

5

The next day, Cora woke up feeling tired and anxious. Drinking, even two glasses of wine, would often result in her feeling more on edge than usual, especially about her health, her boys and Belle.

This sinking feeling of worry would escalate at times to a panic and Cora wasn't far from feeling at her worse this morning.

How silly of her to have had so much in one evening.

She hadn't been drinking for some time and had allowed herself to forget the down sides of it.

Tiredness was not her friend either, as Cora needed a lot of sleep, always had done, and she couldn't have had more than five hours. She somehow needed to find the strength of mind, the calmness that so often abandoned her at the worst possible times, to go ahead with the lunch they had arranged at the Horse and Carriage.

She would be feeling anxious, far worse than she might have done the night before, but she must hide that and push it to the back of her mind. She pondered on whether it would help her most to take Skye for a good fast walk or, to try and sleep for another couple of hrs, but someone's damp and cold nose nudged her arm on the bed and suddenly, the decision had been taken from her.

She had received a text from Rupert, saying that Jill was

resting, and would prefer a visit on Monday, instead of the planned one for that morning, which was such a relief.

Cora hadn't been to that particular pub in years or to many others, for that matter. It was raining hard and she arrived a little late, as she had been keen to find one of her many hats, possibly the least horrid, to wear on the way in. This was to avoid a catastrophic bad hair look, which was so easily achieved by only a few drops of rain and dampness, on what had been a real success the night before.

She ran into the back door of the pub hoping to have a second or two to take her hat off and look at herself in the mirror, one on the way to the bar and restaurant area or the loos; but sadly, that was not to be.

Nicholas and Rupert had taken a table quite close to the door and had called her name the second she had opened it and was in view. Cora had always worried far too much about her hair. She had never liked it apart from when she spent a long time trying to straighten it. So, when not prepared for the occasion and left to follow its wild kinks and shaggy curls, it left her feeling decisively ugly. And today, she couldn't afford to lose courage due to a really 'bad hair day'. She needed all the guts she could find to pull this off, especially as she felt so tired anyway.

Rupert was rather loud again and, although he was kind and charming, Cora started wishing he would allow Nicholas to talk a little more about himself.

She was never going to find out much about him at this rate. An hour and a half later, after a mellow lunch, they left the pub in their separate cars, without any real plan to see each other again.

Cora felt rather deflated. 'So that was that', she thought.

She had probably hoped that Nicholas may have wished to repeat the experience but, realistically, she knew he lived in Ireland, so that was hardly very practical. He had seemingly just been enjoying her company over the last twelve hours. As far as she understood, the pair were going to see Jill the next day, and then travel to London together for the cricket on Tuesday.

Cora felt cold as she parked outside her cottage and walked into her bright kitchen and kissed her dog. Dear Skye, who was never mysterious, or difficult to understand, and always there for her. She felt better already. She would go back to bed for a couple of hours and wake refreshed and ready for some writing.

She hadn't had anything to drink at the pub, and a good sleep would enable her to look at last night's dinner party and today's lunch, with the view of a rational person who enjoys their social life and meeting new people, but who's life doesn't depend on it.

But right now, she just felt low.

Cora lay on her bed, fully clothed and with her duvet pulled right up to her chin. She started to relax, a little, and tried to stop the influx of negative thoughts seeping into her head. It had been a lovely time, the first of many occasions and a very sound first step into normality. 'Why couldn't she just celebrate that,' she thought.

After her split from Sebastian and probably because Cora had put so much into their relationship, she had felt herself turn into a half empty glass person and found it hard to see it any other way. This made her depend hugely on the notion that happiness could only be found, if another created that for her.

Cora had turned much more heavily towards her close bonds

with her girlfriends again, (as so often women tend to do in between boyfriends) hoping to find enough support and love there to not feel the need to replace any of it with another intimate relationship…

She had enjoyed contentment for the last year or so, like a foetus in the 'safe haven' of a mother's womb, very seldom going out or having to deal with any situations which may have made her feel uncomfortable in any way.

But wasn't that the life of someone hiding behind their fears…, and for how long could she realistically carry on like that?

The next week went by quickly, and Cora fell back into her routines. The ones that felt safe and although boring, needed little emotional effort.

She had been to visit her mother who seemed in good health, but she hadn't stayed long as she had prepared an excuse that she needed to leave soon after lunch to take the dog to the vet. She felt a little guilty for telling lies, but she knew that too long spent in Belinda's company would not bring any joy to either of them.

She hadn't heard from Raith which was odd but probably for the best. She still had no idea what he may have wanted from her, so she decided that probably a little too much drink had been consumed and he had texted her in a moment of silliness.

Just as these thoughts were passing through her mind, the telephone rang.

Cora was washing up in the kitchen and, as she picked up her mobile, it slipped out of her hands and fell on the floor. By the time she had retrieved it, whoever it had been, had hung up. She should have dried her hands first. She checked the number and didn't recognise it but called it back anyway. She hadn't spoken to anyone yet that day so even if it turned out to be a sales call, it was always a human being and a little company, even if only short lived, would be quite welcome.

What she most certainly wasn't expecting was to hear Nicholas's voice at the other end. In fact, she was so startled that she nearly pressed 'end' on the call.

He was in the vicinity, after a week in London where he had prolonged his stay because of work he needed to complete there, and was on his way to stay with his sister.

Nicholas wondered whether Cora may like to go out to lunch.

Cora couldn't remember Nicholas ever mentioning a sister…

She really hadn't expected Nicholas to get in touch at all, but the fact that it had taken him a week to do so, could be a positive sign that he was someone who didn't do things impulsively, but thought deeply about them first.

A good thing, considering her own flakiness in the past had done her no favours.

She accepted his kind offer, without seeming too keen, although she would have loved to have replied by saying,

'Thank you, Nicholas, how kind but let me just check my diary', as it was already eleven thirty!

Cora rushed upstairs and chose what to wear carefully and then ran a bath. She had already showered that morning but had been out with Skye and done some weeding and now, felt that a lovely soak in her bath, with some drops of her favourite essential oils, would make her feel like this was a special occasion.

Nicholas was very punctual and, as she sat in his car and looked at him, she was surprised of how really lovely it was to see him again.

He looked back at her as if he was thinking the same, but then he was very subtle, so she didn't want to get her hopes up and start imagining castles in the air.

He drove her to a small restaurant only ten miles away which looked beautiful. Cora had never heard of it which made it even more exciting.

It had a French name, *Le Petit Coeur,* which made it immediately sound delicious and had a pretty garden to the left of it, with a handful of beautifully laid out tables and chairs.

The fact that Nicholas must have done some research and taken obvious care about their lunch date, although seemingly last minute, pleased Cora.

'How did you find out about this gem?' she asked him.

'A little bird told me' he replied with a smile.

Neither of them had spoken very much in the car… he hadn't been shy with Rupert around, so this was a rather different Nicholas she was seeing today.

What of course she didn't know then, was that by the end of that afternoon, Cora had learned quite a lot about his life; one which was in many ways rather surprising, and barely straightforward.

6

Nicholas had never been married. He had a daughter who had been living in Australia with her mother, since three months after her birth. He had spent a night with Sandra Morrison on his gap year, while travelling in Bali, having only met her a few days before. This had not been his usual style at all, but he had been drinking all day with his friends and foolishness had taken over. He had been unlucky.

Sandra had returned to the UK and having managed to trace him down, well before the days of social media, told him she was four months pregnant.

She wanted to keep the baby and was due to move to Australia with her family.

Poor Nicholas had been absolutely shocked by this news; not only because he felt utterly foolish and ashamed for not taking enough precautions to avoid an unwanted pregnancy, but mostly, because of the way she had chosen to deliver this information.

Sandra had been abrupt, short and to the point. She had seemed determined to go ahead with the pregnancy and wished him to have no part in it.

Nicholas was so young at the time, so that after the initial shock had passed, he had resigned himself with the idea that, in many ways, the fact that Sandra was emigrating, sounded like the best solution and he could get on with his life as before.

Or so he had thought.

The truth was quite different.

In the summer following his second year at Exeter University, Nicholas realised that the thought of his unknown and distant child was haunting him constantly, and decided he had to confront it.

Once the decision had been made, he panicked thinking he may have left it too late, having so easily accepted the fait accompli when Sandra had announced her pregnancy and her plans going forward. It had all sounded like the perfect end to a terrible mistake; at least that is the way he had viewed it in his confused and immature mind at the time.

He only had her British telephone number, and no way of knowing where she lived in Australia or, whether she was still there.

Finding Sandra Morrison had been no easy task and very costly but by September, he was sitting on a flight to Queensland to meet his daughter, Selina, for the very first time.

But nothing turned out the way Nicholas had imagined…

Sandra was married and was expecting another child.

She was so young. He wondered whether she had fallen pregnant again, and had married because of it this time…

Sandra had been very unemotional about Nicholas seeing his own daughter, and had been very determined to lay down very clear rules about any future visits, literally from the moment he had walked through the front door of the house, she now shared with her Australian husband.

Sandra's parents had been there too and said hello to him as if he was the person delivering the pizzas. They hadn't engaged in any kind of conversation at all after that.

The whole thing had been so bizarre and unexpected that he felt engulfed in a sea of awful sadness, guilt and anger at himself and spent the following two days close to tears.

He had not been prepared for such coldness. He hadn't been able to spend more than five minutes seeing Selina.

He hadn't, in truth known what to expect exactly, but it had definitely not been this. Sandra had told him that her husband was going to adopt Selina and that she wanted her to grow up believing him to be her biological father.

It was for the best.

She didn't want any financial support from Nicholas, and that he was welcome to visit once a year, if he chose to do so, as Uncle Nicholas from England.

Nothing more.

And that is what he had done for the last thirty-eight years. Selina was now married with three gorgeous children, but his only contact with her was a yearly trip which he took in mid-December, to spend a couple of days with them. Any more would have been against Sandra's rules and considered confusing and disruptive.

This had been incredibly tough on Nicholas and, had had a lasting effect on his life. He had been made to feel as if he had raped Sandra, made to feel like a criminal.

He had been made to feel that he had been the only party to be blamed for what had happened. That he had been very drunk that night in Bali was beyond question, but he knew he would never ever have forced himself on anyone.

Nicholas had hardly stopped talking about his past since they had sat down, and Cora had listened to every word of it.

She suspected that he needed to talk about it and that he

hadn't for a while, if at all…

Cora was starting to understand why this dramatic start to his adult life, might have scarred Nicholas enough to scare him from wishing to make any serious commitments to a woman, let alone having more children.

All of a sudden, she felt terribly sad for him.

Nicholas had made a choice; a brave one; opening-up to her, in such a sincere way, telling her about his past, without asking for any sympathy.

He had told the facts as they were, blaming his own stupidity and naivety for most of the events that followed his time in Bali.

Cora was sitting opposite a man who wasn't saying 'feel sorry for me', and neither was he asking to be helped in anyway.

Nicholas had had a difficult time, but he was someone who showed great inner strength and courage, and spent as much time talking about himself, as he did asking her about her own life. The fact that he had sounded so honest and straight forward to Cora, encouraged her to reciprocate.

Something in her heart told her that if something was ever to come out of this connection, she needed to be completely sincere from the beginning.

Nicholas listened carefully to her talking about her past relationships, without ever interrupting. She nearly stopped a couple of times, wondering whether she hadn't already shocked him into a retreat, especially when admitting that the only way she felt she could protect herself from pain and further hurt, was to be on her own.

That had certainly been her overwhelming view on life over the past year or so.

What Cora failed to see, was what she reflected about herself to others; which was what made her appear so very attractive to Nicholas.

He saw in her a robustness, a resilience, that must have come from years of trying and failing. Of picking yourself up again, and he also sensed an intensity about her, which he suspected came from her taking life too seriously; not necessarily out of choice but need.

After paying the bill, Nicholas looked straight at Cora and took her hand, which had been resting on the table.

She hadn't expected any physical contact at this point, so it took her by surprise, and she nearly pulled it away.

He spoke quietly and gently and said,

'I like you Cora, very much. There is something deeply lovely about you.'

Cora felt happier than she had done for months. Nicholas was different from the men she had formed relationships with before.

He seemed extremely sensitive, caring and understanding without showing the weakness and neediness that most of her past partners had put her through.

While Nicholas was still holding her hand in his, she looked straight into his kind eyes and he continued,

'... however, I am not someone who is going to be able to share with you, the sort of conventional relationship most women wish to have.'

Suddenly Cora's heart seemed to stop for a second. Had she heard him correctly?

Nicholas tried to explain what he meant as kindly as he could. He knew, from Cora's confused expression, that he didn't want to hurt her, especially, as he had been hearing from her how much she had suffered already, at the hands of men in her past relationships, and he had no intention of being next on the list.

Nicholas' life didn't fit well with relationships. He worked for a well-known humanitarian organisation, and travelled a lot, using his parent's house in Ireland, as his bolt hole; but he rarely spent more than a week there at a time. When he could get away, his passion was salmon fishing and he had travelled far for this love, from the Kola Peninsula in Russia, to the Restigouche river in Canada.

Nicholas had so longed to see Cora again, but now regretted their lunch, sensing he had already hurt her by arranging to meet her today and raising her expectations.

He felt awful about it.

What was he thinking?

Cora sat there, feeling blown away.

The closeness she had felt over their time together that afternoon, followed by this admission of Nicholas, saying that he wasn't able to offer anything, seemed to have taken her words away.

She wasn't sure how to respond.

Cora was feeling tired and suddenly anger grew inside her. She had allowed herself to feel so at ease with this man, enough to want to tell him so much about her own experiences, the highs and the lows.

She had believed him to be special, but was she staring at nothing more than an invitation to sleep with him occasionally? Was this what this lunch had been about? She felt like such a fool.

Before she could speak, Nicholas tried to explain.

He had liked her very much at last Saturday's dinner party and had wanted to call her the next day; he had thought about her often since their first meeting, and was disappointed that they had not had the chance to get to know each other better at the lunch with Rupert on the Sunday.

He had reminded himself that meeting her again would only bring her hurt, would be unfair as his life didn't allow for girlfriends as he was always away, and he had got so used to being on his own.

He had formed relationships in the past but although he had made it clear from the start that he didn't want marriage or children, the women that had become partners, and whom had seemed happy to accept this situation, had all eventually changed their mind, and he had found it very upsetting to back out and leave them.

After what had happened to him with Sandra, he just couldn't quite cope with the idea of committing himself to anyone and, although he often dreamt of how life might have been had he married and had had more children, he had opted for the easy way out.

Nicholas didn't see it as a trauma, hadn't ever contemplated going to talk to someone about it and neither did he view himself as someone with a problem.

This had simply been his choice.

His last relationship had ended seven years before and had done so painfully, as his companion, Emma, had been desperate to have a child with him, having told him originally, that she had no intention of ever wanting children.

She had been forty-two when they had broken up, and had

suddenly realised that something huge, was missing from her life and she had not managed to change Nicholas's mind on the subject. Emma had been devastated.

Nicholas had decided then, to close the door on women and relationships and, had thrown himself into his work, his friends and fishing.

Meeting Cora had stirred something new in him, something he couldn't quite recognise, or control.

And more importantly, something he had not in any way, anticipated.

And he liked to be in control of his life and his choices now, that was his shield against making further mistakes; he very much enjoyed being ready for things, especially difficult situations. He liked to be able to have a well thought out plan in mind.

Over lunch, he had liked Cora more and more, and arranging to meet her again, could make it difficult, if not impossible, to set the brakes on anything further happening. He owed it to her and to his own conscience to do the right thing by putting the brakes on now.

Cora had to think quickly; he then wasn't looking for someone to have sex with and no ties, he was looking in fact for nothing to follow their three encounters at all. It felt very strange to her. She had started to fall for him and realised, from how he had explained his point, that, there was nothing she could do to change his mind.

She had felt tired before lunch, but this finale had really taken it out of her…, she suddenly just wanted to lie down.

She wanted to run away, to be back in her cosy house, sitting in her grandmother's blue armchair, with her dog at her feet.

She knew this was going to set her back, but she also recognised that she mustn't allow anger to overwhelm her.

The strength she had gathered together to get through the lunch, the high she had been feeling for the past couple of hours, all to then fall so rapidly as if over a cliff, had proven too much for one day. Now lying heavy on her head was such a wave of confused feelings mixed with the inevitable expectations that all she managed to say was,

'I understand. Thank you for lunch but I now must get back home', and she had disappeared, all before he had remembered that he had driven her there himself. He looked for her by the bar, where he imagined she would be while asking for a taxi, but she had gone.

Nicholas felt foolish and guilty.

Cora had been lucky about finding a lift back.

She had rushed out to the car park, where she had planned to call a taxi, on her mobile, and had noticed one arriving to drop someone off.

Once through the front door of her cottage, she abandoned her tired body in her familiar armchair and burst into tears.

7

The day after her encounter with Nicholas, Cora set about cleaning the house.

While doing so, she purposely played loud music, hoping this would silence or, in the least, diminish the voices in her head.

When she had felt upset in the past, music had formed a kind of barrier for her thoughts and she hoped this would work again.

Cora took Skye to the park and attempted to go about her normal routines as if nothing had happened.

After all, nothing had happened so there was no point making something too big out of this. She would be absolutely fine, just a bit of a misunderstanding. In fact, she reminded herself to call Carol and have a good giggle about it all after she had finished cleaning the house.

Carol was brilliant at putting a funny spin on things and lowering the drama levels, especially as Cora tended to do the opposite. And for a while this technique seemed to play to her wish. Her wish was to forget she had ever met Nicholas, because he had undoubtedly had a big impact on her, and Cora could not afford to allow herself to be dragged down by him.

She had spent such an important year rebuilding her morale, confidence and self-esteem, after feeling totally battered by the breakup of her relationship with Sebastian, that she was so desperate not to go backwards again.

And out of the blue, something unexpected came to her rescue, just at the right time.

Cora's sister, Laura and her husband Colin had rented a house in Spain and that evening, they rang her, offering a last-minute invitation to stay with them for a week.

Someone must have dropped out… Cora thought!

They often took a house in the summer for two or three weeks, but they hadn't asked her to join them for a few years. She wasn't sure whether she felt honoured, or unfortunate, but nonetheless this came at a perfect time.

Even if it meant that she would get caught up with some of the cooking, as had inevitably happened on their last holiday together.

Cora had returned home from that trip, never wanting to have another supper party again, after providing for twelve ravenous people nearly every day for two weeks.

Cora was a fantastic cook and, although it wasn't something she advertised, her sister was well- aware of it. And cooking had never appeared very high on Laura's priority list.

It was the only compliment she could remember her sister ever giving her, and she certainly meant it when it mattered most to her.

Laura was rather manipulative, in that way. Cora was convinced this was one of the reasons why her sister had managed to organise her life exactly the way she had wished it to be, by telling other people what to do and delegating efficiently. Delegating was using the kinder word for it…

Cora had been so quick at accepting Laura's invitation, that she hadn't even enquired who else was going to be out there, but she suddenly realised that it really couldn't have mattered less.

The house was in Palma del Rio, not that far from Córdoba and sounded delightful.

Cora knew she was doing the right thing by getting away, as however much she had tried to convince herself of the opposite, the temptation to go into hiding in her cottage, was strong.

She felt pushed away by Nicholas, rejected.

And even though she recognised that this was for no fault of her own, it still hurt.

A week in the sun, gave her something to look forward to and work towards. She would diet for the next seven days and feel much better by the time she came back with a nice tan.

Cora's journey to the south of Spain had been easy and apart from hiring a car, which ended up by being an incredibly long and tedious process, she felt positive about the week ahead.

The short walk between the airport terminal and the car hire building, had cheered her up.

The sun was warm and there was a light breeze, and she was curious and excited to see what the villa looked like, but as her destination drew closer, Cora started to feel anxious.

She felt her heart racing and stopped the car on the side of the narrow lane, that led up to the rented house.

She needed to regroup her thoughts and calm herself. She was annoyed and upset that these feelings of panic were taking hold of her again.

She felt furious in fact.

She tried to blame Nicholas, in the hope that blaming him would free her of this overwhelming sense of doom that had suddenly returned.

Cora had been looking forward to today and, although the invitation had only materialised a week before, she wanted to spend a happy seven days in the sun, in the company of people who, apart from her sister, were certainly not there to judge her or question her, but just to have a good time.

Cora grabbed the steering wheel with both hands and held it strongly as if wanting to shake it…

She was going to do this… she had to; she had to continue her drive to the house. There was no going back, apart from the fact that her sister and the other guests were probably expecting her to arrive now and had heard the car approaching.

Cora was determined no man was going to get in the way of her thoughts for a very long time to come.

She had allowed Nicholas to stir up feelings in her, new strong unknown ones that were causing Cora to feel submerged by so many anxieties again, ones she had tried so hard to silence.

She started the engine, forced a huge smile on her face, and drove on.

Laura had invited two couples whom Cora had met before and had got on reasonably well with; Lawrence and Priscilla Russell and Tom and Diana Pears. Laura's two children were also there, Henry and Christina, both with a friend each.

The holiday had been fun for the first couple of days, made easier by the fact that Colin and Laura had no knowledge of the recent events in Cora's life which had included of course meeting Nicholas. The sun was beaming down, and Cora felt herself completely relax for the first time in two weeks. She had brought two books with her and was half-way through the first one already, which she was enjoying very much. A light-hearted romance full of humour, was exactly what she needed.

Gradually though things started to change.

The skies clouded over, and rain poured like she had not often seen before. Relentlessly. Cora had to admit that she had never known it so bad on a short trip to Spain in July, so, a trip which had started with high hopes and good laughs, turned extraordinarily quickly into something she didn't wish to be part of at all.

Cora knew her present outlook on life was not terribly positive and it didn't take much to turn her feelings on a downward spiral but nevertheless, as she observed the other guests, she couldn't help feeling that there was something quite fascinating, (although not in a good sense), about watching people's chain of thought when taking a summer holiday somewhere designed for use while the weather is hot and sunny, and how many, turn into rather boring, moaning, and seemingly unintelligent individuals if the weather breaks, hoarding themselves around the house looking quite depressed, totally unable to think about what to do next.

Just to make things worse, Cora found herself suddenly taking on more and more chores, which included most of the cooking. This was not a good omen, and too much a reminder of her last time when on holiday with her sister.

By day five Cora was dying to get back home and was starting to feel more and more like the unfortunate sibling who is still single.

The cosy surroundings of her cottage, Skye's love and the certainty of her everyday routines however dull, were starting to look like heaven on earth.

She checked the weather forecast in Hampshire and she couldn't believe her eyes... twenty-five degrees celsius and sunny!

Everyone had started drinking earlier in the day, far more than while the weather had been good, with the excuse of having little else to do.

By lunchtime this had the unfortunate effect of turning some of the group into loud and over-enthusiastic wanna-be politicians, making all manner of ill-informed statements which was particularly irritating to Cora, who was not only very knowledgeable on the subject, due to her work, but extraordinarily up to date with events in the Commons.

Lawrence and Tom's beliefs belonged to different ends of the political spectrum and neither seemed open to listening to the other's point of view. Both worked in banking, had known each other since university and met up often for lunch in the city, but as their animosity over their political discussions grew, one would have thought they had never met before.

As the subject inevitably fell on Brexit, they seemed to argue their own case louder and louder, rather than debating their opinions in a rational way, which might have been interesting or in the least, entertaining for the rest of the party to listen to.

As these arguments started, which had now turned into a daily routine after breakfast, the women seemed to be happy to initially join in, but then inevitably retreated to their bedrooms to read, to the sound of both the loud opinions from the villa's sitting room, and the pouring rain hitting the windows.

Colin was rather more subdued, but Cora felt this was probably not because of a lack of valid opinions on the matter, but due to fear that Laura would have disapproved of her husband taking part in what was becoming a rather ridiculously loud exchange of views, fuelled by far too many cocktails.

As Cora tended not to drink very much, (well, apart from

very occasionally), her tolerance levels towards others who drank too much on a regular basis was not high, and only exaggerated her now growing resentment towards her sister for having asked her to join them.

She felt, once more, that the main reason she had been asked to Spain, was to help Laura out… doing all the things her sister didn't want to get involved in.

She had suspected that far but had been so desperate to leave home for a change of scene and of course now that she was here, she realised that this wasn't quite the sort of change she needed.

Cora found that during the last five days spent at the villa, rather than trying to befriend Priscilla and Diana further, both of whom were perfectly nice, she allowed her thoughts to focus mainly on the rather tedious behaviour of the male guests.

And she suspected that the reason for this was that their characters and demeanours couldn't have been further from Nicholas's.

And this, of course, made Cora feel increasingly miserable, spending hours 'day-dreaming', about what might have been.

Imagining a holiday with Nicholas in such a beautiful setting, only made her resentment grow stronger, so by the time the seventh day came, her departure date, Cora felt at the end of her tether.

Every word spoken by all the guests, however pleasant, made her wish not to be there.

She wanted to run somewhere, anywhere, away from all the voices in her head.

Cora felt overwhelmed by loneliness.

She was starting to realise that her hopes of forgetting Nicholas by coming out to spend a week in Spain, had not only not come about, but she felt far worse than when she had arrived.

On her journey back to the airport in the hire car, Cora tried to cheer herself up by thinking about her two closest girlfriends.

She felt in great need of their support.

She was devastated about her lack of control over her own feelings for Nicholas.

Devastated at the thought that she had allowed a man to enter her heart, and that in such a very short space of time, he had caused her such distressing consequences.

'How could this have happened? she asked aloud.

She would call Carol and Kitty a soon as she got home and suggest a girlie break in the autumn. When she and Sebastian had split up, both the girls had taken her away for a weekend, which had been such a mixture of outpouring of emotions and overindulgence, that it had felt more beneficial than probably ten sessions with a therapist. The fact that the venue had been a five- star hotel, with the most luxurious of spas only half an hour away from her village, had also helped!

The day Cora left Spain was, of course, absolutely scorchingly hot, which is one thing you don't wish for when you are travelling.

She was the only guest leaving that day, so everyone else was inevitably in a fabulous mood, which was hardly surprising after five miserable days of rain.

Cora wickedly hoped that their good mood would not last too long once they realised they had lost their cook!

By the time she walked through her front door, having suffered a three-hour delay to her flight, it had just gone 6 p.m. and she had sadly missed the kennels deadline pickup time, so Skye would have to spend another night away.

Cora dropped her bag by the mirror in the hall, avoiding a reflection of herself. She was well aware she had made very little effort to look nice when leaving the villa, and the last thing she needed was another emotional knock.

She sat down and quickly went through her mail.

As soon as she took the pack of envelopes that had been collected by her kind cleaner from the floor in her absence, she noticed two handwritten letters.

She didn't recognise the writing and somehow her heart started beating a little faster in anticipation.

Cora's dashed hopes of ever hearing from Nicholas again, were pushed away and were replaced by a sudden and exciting desire to be wrapped up in the warm and romantic expectations of the contents of the letters lying in front of her.

She would open a bottle of wine and pour herself a glass to help her through whatever the letters were to reveal.

She certainly hadn't expected Nicholas to write but a small part of her had so hoped he might.

Cora's mind was galloping ahead of her and imagining what the letters might say…

Nicholas would explain things once more. Regretful of having told her he couldn't ever see her again, he would ask her to go with him on his next fishing trip, having realised that taking a girlfriend fishing with you to Russia could be perfectly plausible and in fact quite romantic. He would tell her that he had just felt terribly scared of hurting her, and then being blamed for it again; he would tell her that he had just got so used to living and being alone, that anything different, at this point in his life seemed pointless.

Cora turned her mobile on silent so to be sure not to be interrupted and was sitting far enough away from the land line for it not to disturb her too, glass of wine in one hand, reading glasses on and ready.

What Cora was to read that evening came as a complete shock.

8

Cora opened both letters at the same time, as she wanted to see immediately whether she had guessed correctly.

But there could be no mistake with regards to the signatures staring at her. The author of both letters was Raith Browne.

Cora sank deep into her grandmother's armchair and felt tears running down her face. She definitely felt over emotional, and she had told herself, she would be a different person in a few days, now that she was back in the safety of her precious home.

What on earth could Raith be writing to her about anyway?

The handwriting was clear and elegant. Cora suspected it had been written with a fountain pen and with great care.

Raith had seemed rather distinguished as well as good-looking and she tried to imagine him writing the letter, sitting at a large antique desk, in front of a beautiful bay window in the Old Rectory in the village.

My dearest Cora, I so wish I could have explained this to you before today, but I never expected we would meet. Not like this anyway and after so many years…

I knew your mother, Belinda. It was many years ago, when we were young. I remember the moment I first saw her as if it was yesterday. She was the most beautiful woman I had ever come across. She was talking to an army friend of mine,

Ian Yardley, at a cocktail party, and laughing loudly at his jokes, throwing her head back. She was wearing a low-cut emerald green dress, with a broad black belt around her tiny waist. The clasp was in the shape of a cheetah's head and I have never forgotten it. She was never one to shy away from drawing attention to herself and she oozed confidence.

I walked up to them, so desperate to meet her, that I forgot my manners and rather rudely interrupted their conversation and introduced myself to her.

My life was never to be the same again.

We fell madly in love very quickly and had a passionate and exciting affair. Nothing about Belinda was usual. She was like no other girl I had met before. Beautiful, intelligent, challenging, sophisticated and often difficult. But always great fun. After nearly two years, I was posted by the army to the East of Suez and then to Northern Ireland and our liaison became too difficult to sustain for her.

I loved your mother deeply but she found life with someone whose first interest was not her, and whose life was often in danger, unacceptable. I struggled desperately trying to keep my career on track and keep Belinda fulfilled but, alas, failed to sustain both. We tragically parted and although not a day went by when I didn't miss her, she never got in touch again.

I very much wanted to have a family and eventually met Helena and we married. She came from an army background and was very much aware of what life married to an officer, entailed. I knew I wasn't deeply in love with her, not like I had been with Belinda, but I believed that I was doing the right thing. Her father was in my regiment and there were many links to our union which made me believe things between us would work out.

After three years, as married life to someone I didn't truly love started taking its toll, I got in touch with your mother again; she in the meantime, possibly to punish me, had married an old school friend of mine, Edward Patterson. I have often wondered what my life, and hers, might have been like, had I not contacted her that day, but it's all in the past now.

We started meeting and our love and passion for each other grew again, even stronger than before. The longing to see one another became nearly unbearable and we found that we couldn't stop our affair. It lasted many years and we both found that the only way to survive our own marriages was to keep our love alive. It kept our hope in life from dying.

Until ten years ago.

I had a son, the second of my children, and he was tragically killed in a car accident. After that, I told Belinda we had to stop seeing each other.

Cora leant back in the armchair and let the letter drop gently on her knees.

The shock of learning about Raith's and her mother's affair, soon turned to sympathy, for him at least, after reading about his son and the tragedy that something like that, must bring to a family.

She was starting to understand Raith's behaviour, on the evening of Jill's dinner party, and it wasn't something she could ever have guessed in a million years.

What he was revealing was certainly something that she needed to reflect deeply over before sharing it with anyone at all.

Cora got up to pour herself another glass of wine and went back to sit down. She had read only two pages of Raith's first letter and had more to come. And why would he be writing a second letter anyway, so soon after the first one?

So many emotions and feelings were cascading into her mind, memories of her childhood, his car which she had noticed driving up to Jill's and the feeling of déjà vu...things were starting to fall into place.

Cora thought back at her parents strained relationship during the last few years before her father's death.

She wondered whether the affair had been able to carry on for so long because in many ways both Belinda and Raith were fully aware that it was all they had chosen to have; from what Raith was saying to her, neither would have left their spouses at the time the affair started or, during it; Raith due to his career prospects in the army and Belinda, because of the financial security Edward had brought to her life; far more than Raith could ever have been able to offer her.

So they had both shown a strong commitment to continue to love each other in this way; but had done so regardless of the hurt and pain which would have engulfed both of their families, had their affair been discovered.

She couldn't quite believe that she had never suspected their affair herself, and that it had lasted through most of Belinda's adult life.

Belinda had, more often than not, shown Cora contempt, handing out harsh criticism to her with regards to her relationships; all of which seemed born from a position of high morals which had always ended up making Cora feel she was severely and, without doubt, at fault.

As Cora tried to put all this together and give it some sense, she started feeling a bit sick. She was so tired but needed to finish what she had started so she read on…

Helena found it incredibly difficult to cope with the death of our son. I decided to take early retirement, only a year before I was due to do so anyway; in the hope that this would help Helena at home and that somehow, we may grow closer. I told Belinda it was over, for ever this time. I told her that I couldn't possibly give my wife the kind of support she desperately needed, while loving her, Belinda, in secret, and we parted.

Your mother took this very badly and showed me incredible bitterness at the time, to the point that she threatened to go to Helena with the truth about our relationship. I had to take that risk, hoping Belinda would find it in her heart to understand and decided to end my relationship with her. I couldn't cope with the pressure both from home and Helena, and had to put my family and what seemed by far the right thing to do, first.

Understandably, Belinda told me she would never forgive me and has never been in touch again. And that was ten years ago.

My relationship with my wife grew closer by consequence, with the softer side of our characters somehow revealing itself to each other, probably for the very first time. Nevertheless, whatever the reason behind it, we are now happier and I am keen for this new-found respect and companionship not to hit any rocks and continue as it is.

The reason why Helena seemed unsettled at Jill's dinner party, had been partly because she had suspected you may be Belinda'a daughter. Only a few minutes before I realised…

We hardly ever spoke about Belinda during our marriage and Helena had never suspected an affair, but she certainly knew that your mother had had a huge impact on my life before marrying me. Helena had brought her name up during difficult times and I think she kept up with news about her through some of my close friends and certainly knew that she had had two girls and knew your names.

Helena remains unaware of Belinda's address or even that she lives in Hampshire. When she called you to let you know that Jill had broken her leg, she had no idea of your surname. But when you were introduced that evening, I am sure, she must have known who you were.

Cora looked up at the time, it was getting very late, but she knew she would never fall asleep after this avalanche of news.

Had Belinda been harbouring hostility and indignation for the last ten years towards a man, who had after all lost his son through tragic consequences? Belinda herself had been determined never to marry him, because she preferred someone who could be there for her all the time, and could give her a far more comfortable life.

Could that have been one of the reasons why her mother had seemed so unhappy with her life and made it her job to make sure everyone shared part of that unhappiness, by being harsh and pretty hard towards people that came across her, whether family or not...?

Cora carried on reading to the bottom of the page…

I am so sorry, Cora, for not being able to tell you all this to your face, as I had planned to do after that evening, but after reflecting on it, I decided that a letter, one which could be read over and over, might be better. I believed it may give you more time to take in all this news.

I so hope you may one day forgive me and understand the extraordinary love that drove your mother and myself to hold on to each other for so long.

I can only hope you have not had a chance to speak to Belinda since meeting me at Jill's as I truly wish to keep our arrival in Hampshire a private one, and maintain my distance now from Belinda as I believe that would be for the best. For all our sakes.

You must wonder why we chose to return to Hampshire, of all places, and I want to explain.

Helena has many friends here, I have too, from the army, so we both felt that we would be happier living close to people we know than venture into the unknown. Of course, I knew that we would be taking a certain degree of risk because of your mother living not too far away, but when we saw the Old Rectory advertised, we felt it was exactly what we were looking for and came to view it. We loved it and put an offer in on the same day.

Helena seemed to have a purpose in life again and I couldn't deny her that happiness and we are excited about the new start ahead of us.

There is more I would like to tell you about your mother, my dear Cora, but for now, I feel I have said enough.

Yours,

Raith

Cora leant back again and closed her eyes. Who wouldn't have wanted to wish the Brownes a happy new life in Mollington, after the tragedy they had being through.

What would have been the benefit of any of this being revealed to her mother, apart from more anguish on both sides no doubt?

Cora had often thought her mother to be quite selfish. The fact that she had not deeply loved her father, but had probably married him for his money, was certainly not something she wished to dwell on at this point of her life. It couldn't possibly bring any real resolve to anyone at all.

People marry for many different reasons, and she was well aware of that. She had never worried about her parent's relationship as a child, or as a young girl when she had been home for the school holidays. They had never openly argued, or not in a way that had caused her any upset, and she remembered her childhood as a happy one.

Cora and Laura had nannies when they were small, or at least until around the time they had been sent to boarding school at thirteen, so she recognised now that her mother would have had numerous opportunities to be away from them and alone with Raith.

Cora was about to open the second letter which had been sent the day before her return from Spain and therefore a week since the first one had been posted. She stopped herself for a moment, sensing that one of the reasons she seemed to be warming to Raith and coming nearly in his defence, was because she had felt rather unloved by Belinda for quite a number of years; in fact, since her divorce.

With her father's death, Cora had felt even more the loss of the kind of love only parents are able to offer. Not necessarily the love and wisdom and good counsel one can also receive from an old special friend, but the love and wisdom of someone who has seen you grow up and change from a little girl, to a teenager and then from a young woman into a mother.

There is something quite unique in that, and Cora felt she genuinely experienced that feeling from Edward. He had been there more as a presence than a natural counsel, but in the bad times, Cora had always felt that she could go to him, and that he would not judge her, but would listen, and gently try and guide her back to where he believed she could manage on her own.

She missed him very much and now even more than she could have imagined. She could have doubted some of the things Raith talked about in his letter, especially when describing her mother, but Cora felt that his view of Belinda, even though he had always loved her very much, reflected the person she knew.

Cora, in fact, wondered whether it was because Belinda refused Raith and married Edward instead, that Raith had found it so difficult to stop his affair with her. It sounded like the never- ending chase for what you can't have, and in a funny way, this had been true for both of them.

Both had probably enjoyed the excitement of something they were aware they could not truly ever call their own, and had maintained their passion through the years.

Cora opened the second letter, hoping this wasn't going to reveal too much more as she was already feeling completely drained with emotion…

Dear Cora,

I am sorry to write again, but I haven't heard from you. I know I asked you not to write but I am now worried that all my news may have upset you terribly. I should have asked you to contact me by text message but I think I hoped you would anyway. I just want to know you are ok.

I know that hardly sounds like a justified request, after everything I have revealed to you, and I understand that my news will inevitably cause consequences. But, please, will you get in touch somehow?

I so hope what you have learned from me will not alter your relationship with your mother, as all she did wrong was to fall in love with a man that was weak. Belinda is an extraordinary woman and although she was very angry with me for ending our relationship, I believe that this was due to the fact that she had relied on my love for such a big part of her life and when I left her, Belinda will have been hugely frightened from the sudden lack of this going forward.

I suspect that she may well have pushed people away since our break up, instead of trying to compensate by finding love from her family and friends. I also fear that this may have been partly caused by her own grief and despair over the lost opportunities to be with the one person she had loved more than any other.

I really don't wish to upset things further by allowing Belinda to find out that we have moved relatively close to her, if I can possibly avoid it.

I want to protect her as much as I do my own family.

So dear Cora, I hope you can find it in yourself to forgive me in time. Please let me know that you are alright.

With love,
Raith

Raith's sympathetic view of Belinda's feelings since their break-up may well of course be correct, but nevertheless, this did not allow Cora to see her mother with gentler eyes... not for now anyway.

She did not show the same aversion towards Laura's life, so, if despair over Raith had made her so unhappy, why had she seemingly taken so much of it out on Cora?

During her life, Cora had had many opportunities to fall out with people close to her. However, she had never been one to hold a grudge, or certainly to the same extent as her mother, or allow herself to be consumed with anger for more than a few weeks at the most.

It was beyond her as to why anyone would want to put so much negative energy into something so ultimately pointless. These revelations didn't make Cora feel that her relationship with Belinda would necessarily change. She would carry on with her policy of keeping herself to herself, where her mother was concerned.

What she believed in her heart would alter, were the feelings she held for her late father, Edward. She now, of course, wondered whether he had truly been unaware of what had been going on under his very nose for so many years.

She suspected not, but that made her feel even more unhappy for him and for his own life, married to her mother.

They did have a rather stiff, and seemingly aloof relationship, in fact, she couldn't now remember any particular sign of affection between them, apart from occasional pecks on the cheek. She had always assumed that it was due to the fact that they were very reserved about intimacy and old fashioned. The need to question it had never crossed her mind before.

The truth, in fact, had been that when Edward had met Belinda, she was so beautiful and entertaining, that he had felt completely bowled over by her. He had never imagined anyone like her ever wishing to be with someone like him, and knew he had to act quickly so he proposed to her within two months of meeting her for the first time.

Although he was from a very wealthy background and became very successful in his own right, he totally lacked self-confidence where women were concerned, and had been terribly shy about meeting girls in the past.

He had always been rather overweight and had lost most of his hair by the time he was thirty, just like his father, and grandfather before him. He was anything but good looking.

But of course, Belinda hadn't cared about that.

Belinda was looking for a kind and generous man and she knew that her union to Edward would bring both. The fact that he was very obviously naive about sex, didn't pose a problem to her as she hadn't wished for any intimacy with anyone other than Raith.

So the Patterson's marriage had never been one of great passion, but Edward and Belinda shared a deep fondness for each other, they had got on well enough and had taken huge joy from the birth of their girls, whom they both adored. But that, thinking back, had changed over time and Cora now wondered whether Raith leaving Belinda might have coincided with the time her parents' marriage started to show signs of deep unhappiness. There had been a sadness which marked that sense of abandonment and resignation, where neither party wishes to, or is prepared to, do anything to change the status quo.

It was now 2 am and she had drunk more than half the bottle of wine, not a particularly nice Tempranillo, but Cora had been in a Spanish sort of mood on her return from her trip, so had opened the first one that had been sitting on the shelf of bottles she kept in the kitchen, rather than in the cellar. These were bottles that she would buy now and again in the supermarket, when on offer, and that she hadn't tried before, but looked promising.

She had always loved her wines and had been lucky enough to grow up with parents who had had a deep love and knowledge of fine wines and, although she was a light drinker, what she did consume, tended to be good.

She suddenly felt utterly exhausted; she needed a long sleep…

Cora would decide in the morning how to reply to Raith.

Although that had sounded like not only a good plan but a very sensible one, she tossed and turned and couldn't sleep at all.

She decided to turn her light on and sit up in bed, and started writing a text with a reply to Raith now.

She wouldn't of course send it till at least ten o'clock in the morning the following day, but she would prepare it and then she could put this evening behind her and move on.

Sending a short text after two letters revealing so much information about oneself, seemed nearly like an insult towards Raith, but there was no other way for her to reach him.

She didn't have his email and neither had he renewed his invitation to meet her for a walk.

Raith had made it very clear that he needed to tell her his story since meeting her at Jill's dinner. He had realised the risk that their encounter, could potentially bring to his efforts to make a new start with Helena in the village.

After much thought she decided to write just two short sentences. The first and overwhelming reason for this was because she didn't quite feel ready to say more at this stage, and secondly, because she wasn't sure she would ever come to discuss this again, with him or anyone else, but wanted to keep that option open.

It read: *Dear Raith, I have been away so only got your letters yesterday. I thank you for your frankness and for letting me know about your situation. I think I understand. Love, Cora.*

She was happy with that. It was a diplomat's reply.

9

Cora was aware she hadn't focused deeply enough on her work in the past few weeks and it had been noted.

She had taken the time in Spain as a complete break and although her commitment to the paper was for one article only per week, she hadn't written as well as she should have done, and she needed to put that right.

For her own sake as well as for her readers.

Cora was a perfectionist and this carried through in the manner in which she wrote, whether it was about the intensity of the research, or the grammar, so when, as had happened lately, her focus had not been a hundred percent on her work, it tormented her.

There was so much going on around the world at the moment, not only at home, that she certainly wasn't short of issues to pick for her piece.

She had written many articles about Brexit over the past three years and was feeling a little deflated with the general mood that this subject was creating. She believed that politicians, from both sides in fact, had underestimated the consequences of the election, and were now going to take at least another year to re-establish themselves, in a way that could lead to a solid following from their supporters again, and prove that their policies were the right ones for them.

One subject that Cora kept close to her heart, but hadn't written about for a while, was the NHS.

There hadn't been much talk lately about the NHS being under continuous pressure due to the number of immigrants entering the country, just more of the same wave of articles about the constant struggle because of under-funding. The issue of immigrants straining the system had been laid to one side since Nigel Farage had made much of it, leading no doubt to his party's success in the EU referendum. She would start with some research on immigrants' numbers into the UK over the past twelve months and go from there.

There had been proposed legislations with regards to the free NHS treatment of EU and non-EU immigrants, but she couldn't recall, whether any of these, had, actually been approved or passed yet. She would focus her mind on work, leaving her little time to think of much else.

Cora was generally good at that; dedicating everything towards a goal and would give it her 100%.

She admitted to herself that since Jill's dinner and meeting Nicholas, she had been distracted… in fact totally absorbed by her many thoughts rather than focusing on reality.

Raith's confession had also added to the basket of what now seemed more like forbidden fruit than much else.

Cora's hopes of receiving some kind of message from Nicholas had disappeared, which was for the best no doubt.

Life back to normal… She worked for most of the next three days and wrote a piece she felt very happy with.

With Skye always at her side, Cora felt she was getting back into her daily routines, so by the end of that week and with an excellent weather forecast for the week-end, she decided to make a trip to a very well stocked garden centre, and make a start on a new herb garden, which she had been planning for ages.

Cora's garden, surprisingly, occupied a far bigger area than one would have imagined a small house like hers to have, and she was very fond of the special outdoor space that had been created by the previous owners. When she had seen the cottage advertised, it was the garden that had particularly caught her eye in the photographs. It had been planned with simplicity, but with a genuine understanding of plants and their flowering times through the year, and colours. The borders were beautiful with blues and whites and pinks taking it in turn to surprise her, with their heads popping up from in between the many shades of green, with an abundance of hostas and grasses in between.

This year she had added some height with beautiful dahlias and further Alliums Nigrum, some cheeky lilac Sanguisorba Tenuifolia Alba, introduced Salvia Patens to lift the softer blues, added more white with more geraniums and scattered some Osteospermum 'Whirligig' as she loved the fun starry shape of the flowers.

The soil was quite acidic, so she was lucky enough to be able to grow camellias and rhododendrons, both of which, reminded her of childhood days spent in her parents's garden.

Cora spent as much time in her garden as she could, and she looked over to the lovely teak bench where she had spent hours, chatting to Belle, over the past few years. They both loved sitting there, discussing how life was progressing for them, in a way that only mothers and daughters that are particularly close, can achieve, by sharing a really special frankness and warmth.

Cora had always been much more of an outdoor person, even as a child, loving plants and animals and every Christmas and birthday, would ask for yet another small pet which, more often than not, was not given to her, as Belinda didn't wish to be left looking after it ,while the girls were away at school.

When she had left home, one of the first things she had done, was to get a dog, which she had not been allowed to have before, and, had never been without one since.

Cora loved looking after people as well as animals. She missed her boys and Belle so much, but she had got used to the fleeting visits now, since all of them had left University.

Ludo had a sweet girlfriend, Bee, who came to stay with him sometimes when he visited home and Francis would still turn up with bags of washing, although he lived in a flat with appliances designed to do just that!

Belle was the most domesticated of her three children, hardly ever arriving at home with anything in need of a wash or repair, in fact she, more often than not, got immediately stuck in, helping Cora with her own daily routines. She had always had a very special connection with her mother; one that allowed them both to understand each other so well, and to often know exactly when the other, needed particular support.

Cora would get so excited when one of them called to announce a visit, but more often than not, it would only be for a couple of nights or three at the most and, before she could take in the smell of their skin and the delight of having them close to her again, they would be off.

So, keeping herself very occupied, was vital to her.

And this became even more important, when she was going through a particularly trying time.

Jill was due home that afternoon from the hospital, with a leg in plaster, and Cora knew that she would probably need quite a bit of help around the house, so she was ready to add that to her 'to do' list.

The next ten days went very quickly as they fell into a routine, which suited Cora well as she could plan and organise her day around it.

Every afternoon she had visited Jill for a couple of hours; not so much to help her as she was doing well but mostly for the company. Jill wasn't able to drive herself anywhere, so Cora's visits were very welcome breaks from the boredom of being stuck inside, with only a handful of visitors and Jenny for company twice a week.

Jill was desperately missing her daughter and her grandchildren, who couldn't come over until Sally's next due holiday from her part time job, which wasn't going to be for another three weeks.

Rupert had been very good about ringing her up every couple of days, but he wasn't planning a visit, which hadn't surprised Cora as, after all, he had just been, and was busy with his job.

Cora had also made a trip to Heathrow to pick up her sister who, in turn, had twisted her ankle badly and, as she didn't want to be seen by a doctor in Spain, had flown back so she could be checked by her own GP and have X-rays etc, if needed.

Colin had stayed out there as everyone else had return flights already booked and the house was paid for.

Laura wasn't a great believer in foreign doctors, which was all rather silly, especially as her injury was hardly life threatening and so many NHS doctors were trained abroad anyway.

Laura had called her sister, under the usual assumption, that she had nothing better to do with her time, than taxi her from the airport back to her house.

Cora had woken up to the most beautifully hot day and had decided to take a lovely bottle of La Grille Pinot Noir Rosé with her, to visit Jill that afternoon. She felt rather sorry for Jill, and wanted to support her as much as possible, knowing very well, that had Cora been the one with a broken leg, Jill would have done exactly the same.

Jill had been delighted at the idea of some wine in the middle of the afternoon, sitting in the deck chairs in the garden. She was utterly fed up with being inside and was all fired up for a good gossip.

After a couple of glasses, Jill seemed to go into 'one thousand questions mode' and a sudden curiosity over her own dinner party, which Cora had managed to avoid talking about, till that day, came flooding out like water breaking over a damn.

Cora had this awful feeling that she was going to deeply regret the original welcome of an afternoon with a gorgeous bottle of wine, let alone the hot sun and found herself in the firing line of Jill's insatiable interrogations.

'What was the food like?', Jill asked. 'Was there enough wine?', followed and so it went on.

Jill then started asking Cora what she had thought of each one of the guests, one by one. She wanted to know whether they had all got on and had anyone noticed the new curtains…

Steering the conversation away from people to interior design, seemed to be working initially but then Cora felt trapped as Jill, turning towards her, asked, 'wasn't Nicholas just adorable?'

Cora suddenly felt rather hot, and a little bit sick but she did manage to say that he seemed very nice.

By this point, Cora felt she needed a glass of water, so she got up with the excuse of needing the loo and went into the house, leaving Jill on her deck chair.

On her way back, Jill heard her footsteps, and before Cora had even sat back in her chair, started asking her about the Brownes.

'Didn't you think Raith was rather dishy?'... 'I bet he is one of those men who got up to no good, while he was posted in the army, and away from home!'

Cora was caught unprepared for this latest comment and so just agreed with her, laughing at the joke.

Jill was particularly interested in the Brownes as they were the new arrivals in the village, and she relished having as much information about anyone who lived close by and who may be interesting enough to mix with socially.

Cora felt she had to give some kind of opinion. She told Jill that Raith seemed very charming, although Helena was a little nervous and shy.

On that note, Cora hoped they could safely move on to a different subject, and she certainly wasn't expecting Jill to enquire any more about that evening.

But Jill was getting a little tipsy, so just as Cora was about to return to her seat with a glass of water for her, Jill said 'it's a shame, my darling that he isn't a widower or single, he could probably do for you, a bit too old mind you... I always seem to forget what a young thing you still are... oh gracious, of course he won't do, he could be your father!'

The force of what Jill had just said hit Cora like a slap across the face, and she suddenly felt very light-headed as if she couldn't quite find her breath; her arms fell by her side losing all their strength and the glass of water fell on the grass; she then clumsily tripped over it, landing on her side on top of her own deck chair. At least she hadn't landed on Jill's leg, causing another injury.

She apologised, and Jill roared with laughter thinking that Cora had had too much to drink and just told her not to worry one bit, as, the glass she had in fact chosen to bring out, was one she most disliked. It was part of a wedding present set and she had always hated the swirly edge on them. Cora wasn't sure whether this was true or not but, she had composed herself again and, after saying sorry another three or four times, took Jill back inside, made her comfortable on her sofa in front of the television, and excused herself, saying she must get back to take Skye for her walk and sober up.

She ran nearly all the way back and as she came through the front door of her house, she slammed it behind her and slumped to the floor.

So many thoughts were rushing through Cora's mind, and she was trying to put them into some order so she could calm down.

The possibility of Raith being her father hadn't entered her imagination before now, but it could so easily be.

She had always thought how like Edward she was, not because she had inherited his looks at all, but because, she had a tendency to put on weight, which annoyingly, Laura didn't suffer from at all. Laura had inherited Belinda's stunning figure.

She quickly tried to think about similarities between herself and Raith. There was nothing particularly obvious… both Raith and Edward had the same colouring, both had dark brown eyes; both were tall with broad shoulders but, where Edward differed from Raith in looks was, mainly his middle. He was definitely, 'on the big side', in fact he had been rather large for most of his life, while Raith, whether by genetics, or due to army life, still seemed extremely fit.

Anyway, speculating at this point was a complete waste of time and would purely produce hours of anguish and to no avail. Her heart was pounding and Cora realised that she was still sitting on the floor, hugging her knees tight to her chest, when she heard her phone ring.

She started to panic and could feel she may be close to one of her anxiety attacks; she opened her handbag, found her lavender oil roll-on stick, applied some to her wrists and forehead and closed her eyes, breathing deeply until she could feel herself relax a little. She didn't worry about missing a call this time.

Her thoughts progressed, but she wanted them to stop. There could be nothing particularly bad to come out of it after all, especially now that Edward had died, but although her rational side could see that, she felt choked with confusion and sadness.

Cora couldn't help wondering whether the possibility that Raith may have been her father, could explain her fraught relationship with her mother.

And if he was, did he even know about it himself?

Having previously decided that she didn't wish to talk to anyone about Raith, Cora realised that she needed to share what he had revealed.

She couldn't quite think rationally enough to trust herself to take a good decision over something quite so important.

However remote this latest possibility may be, Cora now

felt a compelling urge to ring Kitty and to get some advice on what to do next.

She was also unsure whether confronting Belinda was the right answer. Could the reason behind her mother's harshness towards her, be anything to do with the fact that Cora had been Raith and Belinda's love child and that when Raith had left her, ten years ago, Belinda had taken his actions out on the daughter they shared as well as on him?

Or, would such an approach throw her relationship with Belinda into an even worse tsunami of emotions?

She called her reliable and wise friend Kitty, and asked herself to stay for the weekend in London with them.

She hadn't seen her goddaughter Louisa, the middle one of the five siblings, for far too long anyway, so it would be lovely to spend a little time with her too. Kitty had been delighted.

Cora had given nothing away about what was troubling her on the phone. They had all just returned from France, and hadn't planned anything specific for the weekend, apart from a trip to the National Portrait Gallery to see an exhibition of drawings 'From Leonardo to Rembrandt' which Cora liked the sound of too.

Victor and Kitty Davies lived in a lovely house in Gilston Place, just off the Fulham Road, which they'd bought in 1986, two years after they had met. At that point it was a very small terrace house with a tiny garden, but in a great location with the thought that they wouldn't be there for more than a couple of years, before selling on and buying something bigger, further away. After marrying, they had decided to stay and extend by adding another floor to the roof and, as the children kept coming, they had dug into the basement as well.

By the time child number five had appeared, Kitty's career had really taken off and they had been very lucky to be able to buy the house next door, belonging to a lovely elderly lady who had desperately wanted them to have it, so had not even put it on the open market.

The result of all these additions and lots of renovation work over the years that followed, had created the most wonderful family house, with lots of space and light. Cora loved staying there for many reasons, but mainly because it represented something so very different from her own situation. It was always full of noise, laughter and chatting and people coming and going, as you would expect from a household of that size.

It represented so much of what Cora missed now, with living in her cottage, a long way from her children, who were sharing flats in London with their friends.

From Kitty's, Cora could easily walk to beautiful shops, bars, and restaurants. Something seemingly so normal for a life in the city, but so far from the reality of daily life in Mollington.

So every visit to Kitty's in the past, had been a real treat.

Cora had loved those visits.

One of Cora's favourite things to do in London was going to the cinema, which she hardly ever did at home, as it was over an hour round trip to the closest big screen.

She still felt the same excitement arriving at the Fulham Road Cinema, as she had done when she was a teenager.

There was something about the size of the screen, the people around her, waiting for the lights to dim and the whole occasion that made her immediately feel elated, always had done.

Going to watch a film, represented far more than just watching a movie itself... she had always felt immersed in a separate, distinct, world, a happy one without worries or anxieties. One she could lose herself in.

She remembered meeting Stefano there to see the new James Bond movie, and turning up in an old Burberry raincoat wearing nothing underneath it, but lacy underwear and very high heels. She had introduced herself to him as his Bond girl for the night!

He had laughed his head off and couldn't believe Cora had walked from Kitty's house to the cinema wearing practically nothing but a raincoat, especially one which could only be kept closed with a belt rather than buttons, as most of those were missing!

The film had been great fun and he had given her a lift back to the house later, on his bicycle, with her sitting side saddled in front of him, desperately trying to hold on to both sides of the coat from lifting above her knees in the evening wind. It had been November and a very cold one, and one of the happiest evenings she could remember.

Cora doubted she would ever feel so happy and in love again.

She certainly couldn't imagine ever doing something like that again. She couldn't possibly imagine regaining the kind of confidence she must have felt to pull that off... to do something so silly and brave.

And she so missed being foolish and feeling the sort of giddiness which fills every part of your body so to leave no gaps for other emotions to squeeze their way in.

Suddenly another silly occasion sprang to Cora's mind and as she thought of it, she covered her mouth with amused horror; she had been travelling through France with another old flame and he had dared her to remove her t-shirt as a joke, while he was driving, and throw it out of the window, knowing full well that she wouldn't do such a mad thing.

Cora loved a challenge and loved generating laughter and theatre and, although they were on the motorway, she had not only taken her shirt off, but her skirt too.

She had rolled down the car window and checking to see nobody was directly behind them, she had thrown her clothes onto the road and then quickly hidden herself as low down in the seat as she could, in a fit of absolute giggles, leaving her boyfriend in total amused bewilderment.

The laughter and embarrassment that had followed with cars behind them beeping their horns had been quite something and they had joked about it for months.

10

Kitty and Cora had met Victor at Exeter University. Kitty had fallen for him quickly, and had known since very early on, that he was the kind of man she had felt would be right for her.

She was ambitious and knew her own mind.

She was a driven career woman, and one with a nearly insatiable wish to have a very large family, and Victor had met both those desires with 'flying colours'.

He had worked in marketing after leaving university, but had never much liked the traditional 'office' atmosphere, especially as open-plan arrangements were becoming the norm. Also he wasn't a team player, so, eventually, he had found more fulfilment in working from home as a consultant.

This had allowed him to have enough time to look after the children and all their school runs and after school clubs, at least until they had been sent off to board at thirteen. All of them, apart from Leonard, had boarded at schools outside London. Kitty was desperately keen for them to grow up outside the city, surrounded by beautiful countryside.

She wanted them to go to a school that offered as many opportunities as possible, both on the academic side, as well as sports, and her job had allowed them to choose well.

The Davieses had been blessed with bright children who studied well and made the most of their time away from home comforts. Leonard had won a scholarship to Westminster School, after which he had gone on to Cambridge. And all of them had done extremely well. Kitty and Cora often reminded themselves of how very lucky, and immensely proud, they both felt.

All their children had got through school without difficulties, had reached University and had graduated well.

Cora had decided to come to London by train as it saved having to worry about parking.

Her lovely cleaner, Sue, had taken Skye for the weekend, which she did sometimes if she wasn't away staying with her daughter, so Cora had been able to leave, in the knowledge that her beloved dog would be a lot happier than in the kennels.

But she had felt guilty that morning before leaving for London, while trying to finish her piece for the paper. Skye had been particularly needy of her attention, and had jumped up on her knees with her front paws as she often did, lying across Cora 's tummy, and making it really quite impossible for her to see the keyboard, let alone write with it.

Dogs seem to have such a clever way of telling when their owners are going away, and, are about to be left behind.

Cora had only taken a very small bag with her, so she decided to take the tube to Sloane Square and walk down the King's Road, allowing herself to do a bit of window shopping before arriving in Gilston Place.

She walked into the square, facing Peter Jones; this location meant something special for her, tender even, as it was filled with memories. In fact she couldn't think of a single year that had gone by where a trip to this classic department store had not being included, even though she had lived outside London most of her life.

Even now, with online shopping made so easy, Cora still preferred to come here herself and allow the familiar escalator to take her up and down the floors, giving her such a good view of the goods on sale. She delighted herself with looking down at the home decorating displays on the ground floor, with all the many colours, designs, and patterns. She loved all the cushions and felt tempted, each time she was here, to change the colour scheme of her sitting room, just so to give her an excuse to buy some.

Often, she would bump into someone she knew in the store and she found that rather funny, so much so, that she would have a little bet with herself whether it would happen or not. Most of the time, Cora would come away the winner and buy herself something with the imaginary money she had won.

That was a typical example of how light-hearted Cora could be at times considering she had been doing that for years and she realised, most people would think her rather mad for it.

She left Peter Jones behind, walked past York Square, promising herself to come back in the morning for the food market, to see whether an old friend, she had grown up with, might be there with his stall of delicious Italian foods and olive oils.

Cora had walked about four blocks before she suddenly found herself literally staring at someone's back she recognised. It was Rupert, she was sure of it; he stood so close to her, that she could nearly hear him breathe.

She panicked and turned around, to avoid bumping into him, and took a quick turn into a shop. But he had seen her and followed her in, thankfully without realising that she was trying to avoid him.

'Cora, Coraaaa!!' Rupert called, and she turned round, a smile in her face, hiding her true feelings.

Rupert insisted they have a coffee and Cora found herself unable to argue of why she couldn't possibly do this, so they shared a small table on the street, with the warm summer sun shining down on them.

After a couple of minutes, Cora started feeling anxious about how long it would take for Rupert to mention Nicholas, and what he may ask her about him.

Cora couldn't be sure about what information Nicholas might have shared with his friend, if any, but what she did know, was that she didn't really wish to get into a conversation about him at all.

She was here to enjoy her time with Kitty, and her family, and she had already spent the last two weeks, desperately trying to forget ever meeting Nicholas McDonald.

But the conversation took a rather unexpected turn.

Rupert didn't ask her any questions with regards to Nicholas at all which seemed strange especially as gossip certainly ran in the family, and Nicholas and Rupert were very close friends; in fact Cora got the overall impression that Rupert didn't know about their lunch à deux, or showed any signs to make her believe he knew they had liked each other, as much as they had.

He seemed in fact just very interested to know how Jill was getting on; how her leg was progressing as he hadn't had the time to go and see her since his last visit, and, he was very grateful to Cora, for having been so kind towards his sister on a daily basis.

He was hoping to go and stay with her in a couple of weeks,

before going off on his summer holiday.

They had finished drinking their coffee and Cora suddenly realised, time was running out as Rupert was paying the bill, and the silly truth was, that she found herself longing to hear about Nicholas after all.

Cora felt that this may be her only chance…

She wanted to understand more about the reasons that had made him flee from her, without giving her the chance to decide whether she may have accepted to see him now and again; that may have been better than nothing at all. Of course, she recognised that would be a hopeless, painful and ridiculous situation, but nevertheless she had hated the way she had not been given the chance to speak…

Or had she not truly allowed him enough time to explain?

She remembered being so confused, shocked and upset at the time of their last meeting, that all she felt she could do, was flee. But had she been more rational in her view of the situation, may be… just may be, something might have come of it.

Cora had tried to put it out of her mind, and she had kept herself so busy with the garden and Jill and, of course, Raith's extraordinary revelations. But before she could think of the right way to approach the subject, Rupert looked at her and said, 'May I give you a little advice, Cora?'

She didn't quite know what to reply but she said of course as wasn't sure what was to come next.

'I may have read the situation completely wrong, but I believe Nicholas and you liked each other very much, from the moment he entered my sister's dining room that evening. I am not sure what has happened since and how much of what I am going to tell you, you are already aware of, but he has decided to go away for a while.'

Rupert tried to explain, 'I know Nicholas very well and this is highly unusual for him as he is very passionate and so dedicated to his work, but I fear that the reason for it, is because he is so scared that he would end up wanting to see you, if he was here, and that would lead to hurt. I think by leaving, he hopes to put you out of his mind completely, while at the same time try to sort his head out.

Rupert looked at Cora, waiting for her to reply in some way, but she just allowed him to carry on.

'Nicholas has decided to take a six-month sabbatical and he is going to go to South Africa to help in one of the centres that his Charitable Foundation provides financial support for.'

'Dear Cora, I don't believe for one moment that Nicholas would have taken a decision like this unless he felt very strongly towards you indeed.'

Cora sat still, she didn't know what to say. She tried to take in Rupert's latest information about Nicholas, and his thoughts, but couldn't think what to do next.

Her heart felt warm and excited at the concept that Nicholas had truly fallen for her; much more than he had let on. So she had been right about her assumptions with regards to that.

But her mind felt upset, even angry at the thought that he was planning to leave the country in order to avoid, and, forget her altogether.

She told Rupert that she felt that Nicholas was possibly running away from himself, from the fear of getting hurt as much as he was from the fear of hurting other people. She had liked him very much and had been very sad to see it all end, before anything had really been given the chance to take off.

But Nicholas seemed very strong minded and very sure about what he wanted in his life, and what he would rather keep out, and Cora couldn't see how she could change his opinion on that. Neither did she believe that trying to do so was the right approach or, that it would in any way, form a good foundation for any relationship at all.

As Rupert started replying, Cora was aware that the coffee shop was filling up and they had finished a little while ago, and people were queuing up waiting for a free table. There is nothing worse than trying to have a private conversation, while a group of people are hovering around you, hoping they may annoy you enough for you to leave.

This made her feel unsettled, and she asked Rupert if they could leave and walk together for a few minutes. As they started heading towards World's End, Rupert stopped and said,' I am a great believer in fate but sometimes you have to help it along a little. Nicholas is my closest friend and he hasn't been happy for a long, long time.'

Rupert was silent for a moment then added: 'he muddles through and he has learned to live with life as it is: locking out anything that may be viewed by him as a risk to his safe routine, but I saw how you made him feel and he was incredibly happy around you. He is such a decent man, but one who is scared. Throwing himself into charity work in South Africa is very honourable, but what he is actually doing is punishing himself for having allowed his emotions to run wild again, but I think it is madness. He hasn't loved anyone for ages now and he pretends that is what he wants.'

'Can I ask you a very personal question and of course you don't have to answer at all,' continued Rupert… 'How do you feel about him? Did you feel a connection with him?' he asked.

One thing Cora could not accuse her life of being right now, and that was boring.

Between Raith and Nicholas, there was enough to be going on for quite a long time.

'I definitely felt a connection with Nicholas and yes, would have loved it if he had proposed to see me again, but I was so taken aback by his behaviour, that I had put any hopes of that happening to one side, if not behind me, altogether.' Cora replied.

To learn what she had today from Rupert, had opened up the 'market- place' of her emotions again.

What was he recommending her to do?

In her past relationships, Cora felt that she had definitely been the driver, the conductor, and the ticket collector. One thing that she was very keen to avoid next time round.

She told Rupert therefore that she believed that if Nicholas had strong enough feelings for her, he needed to work that out in his own mind, without anybody's help or advice. She didn't think she should be the one to stop him going away, if that was what he truly believed, was the right thing for him to do.

If those feelings were still alive and strong six months on, then he might come to another conclusion about what to do next, rather that running away and trying to choke his emotions.

But surely that had to come from him and him alone?

Cora couldn't quite believe she was saying this.

She could safely say that no man had ever loved her enough to feel that he needed to leave his job, and the country, and fly to Africa, in order to forget all about her.

This was a first, and it made her feel quite special and honoured. In fact, the whole idea sounded rather romantic to her in a naive kind of way, especially as she couldn't see how Nicholas's being in another country, could bring her any happiness at all.

Cora knew this was the only sensible advice and one she would give any good friend of hers, although not something she would have necessarily taken on herself in the past.

She felt completely surprised at herself for not letting her feelings for Nicholas run away with her, and, for sounding so wise in the matter. Was she going to regret this within half an hour?

Was part of this new way of looking at a potential romance, a consequence of what Raith had revealed to her?

Rupert seemed surprised at first but then told her he admired her strength and what she had said; a telling sign, he thought, that she was a truly lovely person.

That made Cora feel slightly better.

A compliment when you have just said something you may live to regret dearly was very welcome… or was it just madness?

Rupert then added that if Cora and Nicholas, were ever to work things out, his dear friend, would be a very, very lucky man. They said their goodbyes and promised to meet up again in a couple of weeks, when he returned to Hampshire, to stay with Jill.

Her encounter with Rupert had put Cora truly off the frivolities of window shopping, as her head was swirling around with too many thoughts and probabilities. She decided to take a taxi to Kitty's, as there was just so much to say to her. But when she got there, the house was so full of people and chatter that she didn't get a chance to be alone with Kitty until the next morning. This gave her the time to put her case into some kind of order, rather than it being a miss mash of too many things, too quickly. She chose to start with Raith.

Victor had left at 9 a.m., with the two boys to play tennis at the Hurlingham, and they weren't going to be returning for at least a couple of hours, while the girls were still asleep. Once Cora had explained everything that had happened with regards to Raith, she decided, for some reason, that she would not approach the subject of Nicholas yet.

She wasn't quite sure why this was, but she assumed that it may be because she hadn't absolutely decided that she was going to be able to fully adhere to her own advice, and didn't really want to hear a similar suggestion from Kitty.

This would only make it more awkward if she chose to take a different path, from the one she had shared with Rupert.

Cora needed more time to think about yesterday and she could only do so when she returned home. This visit needed to be about getting help from her close friend with regards to Raith, his revelations, his request and her mother. First and foremost.

11

Kitty's reaction to the news of Raith's presence in her friend's life was as pragmatic as Cora had expected; do nothing. She didn't see the benefit of presenting these facts to Belinda or challenging her about it, as she suspected that Cora's mother would react very harshly to it, with the possibility, that their already strained relationship, would take a turn for the worse.

'It's been too long, and she has shown such a contrary attitude towards you for many years now that the reality of her admitting her wrongdoing is highly unlikely,' Kitty had said.

Even if Raith was her father, and the loss of him had made Belinda reject her daughter's love in the way that she had demonstrated so clearly, she just couldn't imagine Belinda would ever recognise her own obvious lack of sensitivity and affection, let alone, how truly unjustified and cruel she had been towards her.

The circumstances of her birth were not her, Cora's, fault, Cora felt. If that had been the truth, perhaps they were better forgotten and left alone. Cora accepted Kitty's judgement but did so with a heavy heart.

She tried to digest what was being said to her and, on the whole, agreed with Kitty, but the one question she had, was, who was her father?

Would she spend the rest of her life, wondering?

Didn't she have a right to know, especially as one of the

people in question was dead and the other one had just moved into her village?

Kitty was probably right with regards to her mother. Cora couldn't quite see how Belinda's behaviour, in relation to her, would ever change.

But should she not try and find out who her father was, and could she not attempt to do so, without involving her mother?

If she did conclude that Raith was, indeed, her father, what effect would it have on his life, and what of his relationships within his own family?

Cora had a lot to take into consideration before doing anything at all about this chapter of her life.

It was indeed like staring at a very valuable book, opened two thirds of the way through, and wanting to go back and be able to read what happened at the start, without being altogether sure that she had the courage to then cope with what would follow.

Her weekend in London continued as planned, with lots of time spent with Victor and Kitty and some of the children. She hadn't managed to spend as much quality time with Louisa as she had hoped, mainly because Cora's arrival had been a very last minute idea and her goddaughter had already made plans to be out with friends, but she had promised her a special shopping trip next time she was in town and that seemed to go down well. Victor's brother was in London working for a week, so the four of them went out to a sweet Italian restaurant in Hollywood Road for dinner, on Saturday night, which was a lovely treat.

Cora felt very jealous of the fact that they could walk to lovely restaurants and could enjoy a busy social life, so close by, and longed for more of it, but she knew that once back in her cottage, she would cherish that life too.

Cora would have loved a tiny flat in London and would have used it often, but she certainly couldn't afford to have two houses. She had considered moving there quite a few times through her life, mainly just after the end of a relationship, when she felt at her lowest and most isolated, but had resisted and in many ways, was glad she had.

There was a big part of her that valued her village life so much now; the freedom of her garden and having Skye with her as her constant companion, who could just wonder around without any fear of getting run over or needing to be taken to a park if she lived on the fourth floor of an apartment block, a long way from any sort of green space. Since moving to Mollington, she had felt such a sense of community. She had been made to feel so welcome and, for now, couldn't imagine swapping that, for life in a big city.

Cora wouldn't say no to a tiny studio flat near Kitty, that would be wonderful, where she could come and go may be once a fortnight, for two or three days to see the children, catch a show or a film and an exhibition. Yes... that would have been nothing short of a miracle.

Just as she was preparing to say her thank you's to the Davieses, she received a text message from Francis. He wanted to come and stay that night and apologised for the late notice.

Cora adored her children but, somehow, she wasn't sure she was ready to face any of them quite so soon, after all the news she had received lately, and so wished she could have had a little more time to think.

She could have easily replied she was going to be in London

another night but she couldn't bear to lie to him and hadn't seen him for nearly two months. May be seeing her eldest son, would help her put all this into perspective… a reminder that all that truly matters is what is ahead of you, not what's happened in the past.

She didn't ask what time he was arriving, just wrote back telling him she would see him for supper as she was just leaving London. She said her goodbyes and hailed a taxi for Waterloo. Cora sat on the train and felt quite jumpy.

The present was all starting to feel a bit overwhelming and this state of mind was exactly what she recognised to be a place she shouldn't be venturing in… to feel over anxious was what she had battled so hard to free her life of, and in the last year she had created a safe bubble around her where things were, on the whole, much calmer, and reasonably relaxed, and this had taken a lot of emotional effort and time.

One thing she had learned was that often the best way forward was to take decisions sooner rather than later so she endeavoured to do just that, both with regards to Raith and Nicholas.

Leaving any unresolved issues would only bring further panic into her life. That thought made her feel infinitely better already, although of course, she didn't quite know yet what those decisions would be.

There was absolutely no point in making her life worse than it had been in the past, and Cora reminded herself that she wanted to be in control of any decision she made from here on.

If Nicholas liked her so much, let him go off to Africa and work it out, or not. He could return after six months, if he chose to, and ask her out properly. Anything less, wasn't worth her while; her life was too complicated already.

Making a plan of action, with regards to Nicholas, made Cora feel decisive and stronger.

But what now of Raith?

She could do nothing like Kitty advised, or she could take the bull by its horns, and confront either him or Belinda about her doubts over who her father was, and then go from there.

In many ways, she had been so upset with her mother over the past few years, that challenging her about something like this, felt rather satisfying.

Belinda had spent so much time criticising Cora over her own life choices, especially where relationships were concerned, that a small part of her, now felt it was her turn to hit back... Cora of course knew that this thought of hitting back at her mother, was hardly kind, or well-meaning, but something deep inside her soul, which had been there a long time, made it hard for her to think straight.

Tonight she would just focus on having a lovely evening with Francis, hear all about him and what he had being getting up to since she last saw him, tell him how much she had enjoyed London, and seeing all the Davieses, and find out what had brought him to Hampshire on a Sunday evening at short notice.

As that thought passed quickly through her mind, Cora paused and started worrying that he may not be well, or that something may be wrong with his work or even Belle, or Ludo, and he was coming to bring bad news, being the eldest, but she mustn't allow her silly mind to steer her in that direction, she knew too well what the consequences of that chain of thought would cause. She was tired and stressed by everything that had hit her over the past two weeks; she was just over thinking things and panicking.

Cora recognised this emotional pattern and desperately hoped that she hadn't let things slip downhill too much.

She must try and get more sleep and make time for her twenty-minute daily meditation sessions again. They were always such a support to her and most of the time, truly helped her put things in the right prospective and induce calm.

Cora never slept very well away from home, and, this weekend, had been no exception. Tiredness was one of her worst enemies. By tomorrow morning everything would seem a little better, far less of a burden, and quite resolvable.

Francis was in great form, he had grown his hair and soft blonde waves now framed his striking angular face, just like Mark had worn when they had first met.

Cora felt so proud of her boys and Belle. Ludo was more of a Patterson, darker and skinnier, with narrow hips and long limbs and a confident, jokey manner. Francis had his father's long back and light skin and fair hair, but Cora's sensitive, generous and, slightly insecure character. Belle was a good mixture of both her parents, with what was best about them in many ways.

Francis had been asked to attend a conference on Monday in Salisbury by his firm in the city, but had completely forgotten about it until yesterday, when he had checked his diary for the coming week, and had hoped he could stay the night with Cora, to break up the journey.

Although the cottage in Mollington wasn't where the boys and Belle had grown up, they still considered it home as they seldom stayed with their father. Nearly everything Francis could lay his eyes on in the cottage, was familiar to him, and it felt warm and homely, so he cherished coming down to see

Cora. She had always made a big effort to create a nest for the children, a welcoming home to come back to, whenever they felt like it.

Their bedrooms were full of pictures; from ones that had hanged in their nursery as babies, all the way throughout their school days, nearly every year of their time there.

Francis did notice that Cora, wasn't quite as relaxed as she had been on his last visit, but he wasn't going to worry about it too much, as he knew his mother well and knew she overly worried about the smallest things.

He also knew that she had an extraordinary strength that had seen her through the hardest of periods, and he was sure that would always be the case.

Cora knew that often, it is the children of parents who seem to have gone through the most troubled times, that end up having an assumed view of them as 'super', nearly divine human beings, and somehow invincible.

Francis felt that if his mother had had something particularly troublesome on her mind, she would have told him… he was sure of it, as they were close.

They didn't have a late night, as he needed to leave early, and Cora was tired, although she didn't admit to it, but he could tell.

The next morning, after Francis had left, Cora walked up to Jill's house to make sure she was ok, but as she came around the corner, past her little garden gate, she saw the open top Jaguar. Since Raith's revelations, she was nearly sure, that the reason why she had felt a sort of connection with the car, on the evening of the dinner party, must be because she must have seen it often while she was growing up, but had never realised who it belonged to… probably parked near her parent's house, when Raith was sneaking in to see Belinda.

She stopped to decide whether to go in or come back later. She decided on the latter, but she got caught out by Jenny coming out of the house. She had done her three hours and was on her way to help another one of her clients in Mollington.

Jenny, although very humble in her manner, had a rather loud voice, so there was going to be little chance of avoiding being heard by Jill and her guests on this occasion. After a brief chat to Jenny, Cora felt therefore she had to walk into the house, and followed the voices through into the drawing room.

It was a warm day, and the new wide French windows were open, letting in the heat from the sun.

Raith and Helena were sitting having a cup of coffee and chatting away about their recent trip to London, also apparently the weekend that had just passed.

Cora joined them, not having a clue about how to greet Raith, or how to behave naturally in front of him, or Helena for that matter. He quickly read her thoughts and was reassuringly affectionate this time, kissing her on both cheeks, with his arm gently holding her back, very different from their first flirty encounter.

They all sat down again, and Cora stayed for only half an hour, as she just couldn't quite get her head round how weird it all felt.

Helena had avoided looking straight at Cora but hadn't altogether been unfriendly… just a bit cool.

Cora's caring side truly felt for her, although she was unsure of how to reach out to her in any practical way. Helena had been caught in between Raith and Belinda, through no fault of her own. She had suffered most, no doubt, from being in a loveless marriage, to the sudden death of her son.

All those reasons seem not only to draw Cora towards her, wanting to show a certain degree of empathy for this quiet and delicate looking woman, but somehow to protect Helena from further hurt.

Something inside Cora wished she could have taken Helena to one side and told her she understood, told her that she was feeling so hurt too, but that was totally unrealistic.

Cora learned that the Brownes had a small flat in Pimlico which they kept very much as a pied à terre, and used only about once a month for a few days, to catch a play or go to art exhibitions.

They would always try and include a visit to their daughter Lucy, who had just moved with her husband to a lovely house on Camberwell Grove, and to their youngest son, Peter, who spent weekdays in London, before returning to Shropshire at the weekends.

They had all in fact been to the same exhibition that weekend in London, and the two women spoke about their love of drawings and then went on to chat about their dogs, and what amazing company they had been, especially at stressful times in their lives.

Cora couldn't help herself peeking at Raith above Helena's head when she wasn't looking her way, hoping this would go completely unnoticed, especially as the last thing she wanted to cause, was any more concern.

Could she spot any obvious resemblance with her potential father…nose, cheekbones, hands…?

She wondered how often Lucy came up to visit, as she

thought that this could be another way of trying to work out, whether the 'two daughters' were anything like each other. Ridiculous thoughts entered her mind about returning to London and walking up and down Lucy's street trying to spot her going into, or leaving her house...was Camberwell Grove a long road?

Was it doable?

Was she going mad?

The answer to that was: yes, probably.

But Cora knew that however mad she may or not be, these thoughts were not going to pass. They were not going to go away.

She knew Kitty was right to some extent; from a very practical point of view, yes, she was absolutely right but, at the same time, Cora wasn't, in any way, convinced that her great friend could grasp the meaning of not knowing where you have come from.

This had to be resolved in one way or another.

That evening she had a long chat on the phone with Ludo, who was in flying form, as he had just been asked to join a group of friends sailing, off the Croatian coast. Cora suspected that one of them would be Bee, his girlfriend of over two years now, although Ludo was very diplomatic over the release of intimate information about his life, probably as a result of their mother having been the opposite during the past twenty years.

Cora had never wanted to keep secrets from them although looking back on things, now more than ever, she recognised that at times, she had in fact overloaded them with so much honesty, that they often used to let the information just go over their head, to keep some normality over their day to day lives.

Cora had been careful not to talk badly about Mark, most of the time, over the years, which had certainly helped maintain a very good relationship between father and sons. Belle wasn't as close to Mark as he would have wished. She was too close to Cora, not to hold some blame on her father, for their marriage break-up. She was also the strongest, and the most opinionated of the three.

Cora was delighted though, that all the children felt that they could openly chat about their father in their mother's presence, knowing that Cora had moved on with hers and wouldn't resent him being happy with someone else.

It still seemed very strange to Cora not to have much more contact with her children.

She missed their company every single day.

She missed not being able to kiss them and hug them and feel closer to them.

The realisation that they now had their own lives, away from her, mostly detached from hers, had been a difficult process.

Cora appreciated why she found this particularly hard… she knew the lack of continuity in her love life, was partly to blame. Even when Cora was with Sebastian, in the early days, she remembered that he didn't seem to sense the hollow she had started to feel, since the children had left home. Cora probably didn't want to talk about it very much, as he had no children of his own, and she didn't want to sound as if his love alone, wasn't enough to make her feel cared for.

But then Cora had never expected to feel such emptiness.

12

Cora knew mothers who felt completely lost in the first few months of their children going to university, especially her friends whose children had not been away at school like her own.

But although she had been well trained in the art of being at home without them since they were thirteen, when Francis, Belle and Ludo had moved to work and live in London, it had felt very unsettling for her.

When children were at school and university, parents could still rely, by and large, on those guaranteed times when they would be returning home. It was part of a well-designed plan for months ahead. Now, Cora's children's visits, mostly, took place when work and friends or, girlfriends and boyfriends, allowed, and at times, Cora had felt that they may be returning to the nest more out of duty than a longing to see her.

They had built nests elsewhere… but Cora knew that she felt this emptiness, this kind of lack of purpose, in an exceptionally raw form because she was alone.

Skye was looking at her while these thoughts were rushing through her mind, and with such a soft and gentle expression as if to say, 'I know exactly what you are thinking, but you are hardly alone, you have me!'

And, of course she was right.

When sad thoughts entered Cora's mind, she knew that she needed to replace those quickly with happy and grateful ones and she did so now.

And Cora had so much to be grateful for.

Her two beautiful boys were happy and healthy; Belle was pretty and so full of life and excited about her future. All three of them seemed to have lots of wonderful and loyal friends, from their school days, university and more recently, connected to their jobs.

What more could she possibly ask for?

Anything extra was just a bonus and bonuses were just the small branches of a terrific tree which she had created.

Every year, the tree of life seemed to flower, and then shed all its leaves; just like in real life, her own life, which had been full of ups and downs. Often much more like a succession of windy autumns, harsh winters and wet summers.

Some years, circumstances had been undeniably unkind to her, but, on the whole, she had not only survived but thrived once more, just like the fruit trees in her garden, with fresh beautiful blooms and the greenest of leaves.

Cora remembered a very hard winter, four years before, where the garden had suffered badly, both from extreme rain and wind, and she had been devastated at the thought of losing some of the trees and plants she had so carefully looked after and enjoyed.

But most of her garden had shown great fortitude and within a couple of years, was looking wonderful again.

Cora used to compare her break-up with Sebastian, to a natural disaster, where no loss of life has come about, but where, nevertheless, an enormous amount of effort and work has to go into restoring things back to how they were.

Cora's thoughts went back to three weeks ago...

She knew she had reached a better place, which was not to mean that she hadn't altogether been aware that she was still vulnerable and, meeting Nicholas and Raith, had thrown her life completely upside down.

Raith seem to represent a grey cloud in what had been her path to rebuilding her life for the past year, and she didn't mean that in a nasty way at all, but Cora truly believed now that she needed to resolve this subject rather than brush it to one side, desperately hoping that it wasn't going to bring a huge deluge down with it.

Cora had been brought up as a Catholic and so had Francis, Belle and Ludo, but she seldom turned to religion for support nowadays. She hadn't necessarily questioned or challenged her beliefs, but neither did she think that adhering to the Church in a more prominent and regular way, was going to be of any help to her.

Where or when this passive approach had first made its way in her mind, Cora wasn't entirely sure, especially as both her parents had been regular church attendants, but she sensed it may have generated out of years of writing about wars and religious conflicts around the world.

Cora did see herself as a deeply spiritual person.

She believed in the importance of having someone better and bigger than ourselves to guide us and to look up to; she just wasn't entirely sure, whether that was a Christian God.

She had learned about other doctrines which had helped her along the way, and she liked being energised by people who served as great examples of doing true good on earth, whether that was Mother Theresa, or, someone totally unknown to most. Her spiritual energy, often stemmed from people she knew, or had known personally, who had shown outstanding kindness, understanding and generosity towards others.

What mattered to her was what these people had shown to do, with their actions rather than just words.

One of these, was her maternal grandmother, whom had died on the same year as her father and whose photograph, Cora always kept with her by her bedside table. It was a small photograph of her with Francis as a baby in her arms. She had come to believe that her grandmother protected her and when things had been particularly difficult in Cora's life, the photograph in the small gentle frame, would accompany her in her handbag.

When Cora had experienced health scares in the past, which would cause her great anxiety, her grandmother's photograph would be in her bag and she would kiss it before going in to see any consultant or before any test, believing in her mind that this would help her hugely to get through whatever was to come next.

The boys and Belle had been christened, had received their First Communion, and had been confirmed, and she had never regretted offering them, the first steps towards a Catholic upbringing, but she also believed that what they chose to do now, was completely up to them, and she respected that without any judgement.

Cora suspected that they would probably make church going, a handful of times per year occasion, while maintaining respect for the religion they had been brought up into and she hoped, full tolerance of all others.

With thoughts of religion flowing through her mind, Cora dwelled on the one thing she found difficult to tolerate in life: lies.

This reminded her of the situation with Raith and Belinda.

She also thought back at her own experience with Stefano and, although he had not been divorced, at least they had very much planned a future together, and that had been her full understanding of what would ultimately follow their hidden rendezvous.

But they had lied too.

He to his wife, and Cora to her children, although only initially, in fear of hurting them with the truth.

So, what made Cora believe that her mother and Raith were any worse?

She couldn't quite imagine deceit of the magnitude that Raith and Belinda had embraced, mainly because they seem to be completely aware of their plan, one that seems to have no destination, one where reaching a place where they would stop cheating on their respective partners, had never been a priority. And it was a plan that went on for so many years, and that had Raith's son not died, they would have followed through till the end.

Cora felt so cheated about not knowing.

Wouldn't it be better for the truth to come out, at least within her own family as she didn't wish to bring any more pain to Helena? Could she confront her mother and make sure that this well-kept secret, at least of their affair, stayed within Patterson walls and not filter further?

If she was to find out that she was in fact, not Edward's daughter, how would that change her life, and would she want to play a part in Raith's? Because surely that was out of the question…

That evening, Cora took a huge decision. She would drive to her mother's, the next morning, with no warning, and confront her; both about the affair, and, the possibility of Raith being her father.

She would ask her both questions, without resentment or judgement, as she realised that in many ways, she had no right to approach this cause in such a manner. At the same time, she knew that the main reason she was doing it, was that she needed to find out the truth.

Cora needed to know… she wasn't even sure whether it mattered to her more to find out who her father was, or to understand why her mother had been so harsh on her for at least ten years. She had learned to deal with it well of course, but all that meant, was that she avoided Belinda in as much as she could. Cora stuck to her dutiful visits, which was how she could make absolutely sure Belinda was in good health, nothing more.

She was past the point of thinking about how Belinda may have reacted, in fact she made a real effort not to even think about that now, as all she was interested in was the truth that had been hidden from her for such a long time.

She was going to do this.

It was going to happen, and she would have to explain to Kitty later, why she had, so fiercely, decided to go against all her advice.

Cora got up the next morning and took her dog for a good walk, as she wasn't sure how long she would be away from the cottage that day.

It was raining hard which was not a good premonition and

she'd already had a few moments of indecision since she had woken, wondering whether she would live to regret what she had set herself out to do later in the morning.

Skye had chased a dog in the park, of all days, with the intention of only playing with it, as she didn't have a cruel bone in her body. Sadly, the dog's owner, who Cora had never seen before, hadn't taken well to this game. The dog did look rather like a baby rabbit, so it was hardly surprising Skye had got so excited!

She wouldn't have harmed it of course but the owner didn't know that at the time, so Cora spent ten minutes apologising and trying to drag Skye home, having forgotten the lead, which she seldom brought with her these days.

She went to change her trousers, which were now covered in mud, and contemplated having a swig of brandy with her toast.

Not something she had ever done in her life, but maybe it would help. She didn't even know whether she would like it as she only remembered using it in puddings, but somehow gin or vodka seemed far worse an idea at that time of the day, and she hated whisky.

By half past ten, Cora was driving through her mother's village heading for her driveway, but something caught her eye.

It couldn't be... surely? thought Cora.

She had to stop and park and just make sure she wasn't going mad. She took a few deep breaths, hoping the vision of a few moments before would just disappear, but it hadn't.

She was looking through her rear mirror now, and she could clearly see Raith's car, parked by the church.

What on earth was he doing here??

Could this be a pure coincidence... he could have a friend

in the same village. Yes, that must be the reason, she mustn't jump to conclusion, she was being ridiculous.

Quite neurotic in fact. She realised that she was starting to lose her nerve.

The village wasn't small and was well known, with a good number of lovely shops, so it might have easily been Helena visiting the interior design store on the High Street, the one Belinda had so often spoken about.

Cora, suddenly felt all her courage evaporate, and having lost the strength of mind to follow through her intention, drove home.

By the time she was sitting in her kitchen again, having a cup of her favourite fennel tea, she felt safe and calm again. She realised that unless she was completely ready to challenge Belinda about her affair with Raith, she shouldn't attempt the journey again.

The reason she had turned back today was obviously a sign she wasn't quite ready for the consequences, and she should wait till she was stronger and, better able to approach the whole issue, especially, as it was likely to be a very bumpy ride.

So, she could thank Helena, and the interior design store, for stopping her in her stride this time. It made her realise that Raith's poor wife, couldn't possibly have imagined that Belinda lived in the same village, as she wouldn't have set foot in it.

That evening Cora rang Kitty and told her what had happened. She hated the idea of lying to her closest friend, even more than she did of going against her advice, so she was glad to 'own-up'- to her actions.

Kitty hadn't been altogether surprised as she knew her best friend well, and knew what a strong determined soul she was.

She did ask her why she hadn't waited where she had parked her car to see who the driver of the E-type had been earlier… but Cora admitted that she had been far too scared to find out, and had left in a hurry, in the hope that she wouldn't suddenly be facing Raith, rather than Helena.

This worried Kitty and she told Cora so. This was already getting out of hand, exactly the reason she had tried to put Cora off investigating the affair in the first place.

Kitty feared, that Cora was putting herself in a situation, that may well lead to a position where back tracking would become impossible.

She also sensed that Raith may be lying to Cora with regards to making a fresh start at life with his wife in Mollingon, especially, as he seemed very keen in his letter, to stress the importance that Helena, should remain totally protected from the truth.

Kitty worried that this whole affair would only bring back a huge amount of stress and anxiety in Cora' life, emotions that she had just spent the last year working so hard to diminish.

Kitty would do anything not to see Cora return to the person she had been this time twelve months ago. Before they could continue their conversation, Louisa had stormed into the kitchen, having heard her mother on the phone with Cora, and wanted to talk to her about what she had finally decided she would love her godmother to give her for her birthday.

Cora didn't speak to Kitty for nearly a week after that which was quite a long pause for them.

This was mainly due to embarrassment, for having gone ahead with something her friend had advised her not to do.

It was also, partly, because she realised that these thoughts of Raith's whereabouts, in her mother's village that day, were starting to take over most of her life, which was leading her down a negative path.

Cora felt that a distraction, however silly, was what she needed right now… she was spending too much time on her own, and her one piece a week for the newspaper was just not enough to keep her mind occupied, let alone from straying into territory that was unknown and dangerous.

Then suddenly, something quite mad and highly risky, appeared in Cora's mind…

13

What Cora had failed to see was that there was a solution to achieving a break from issues surrounding Raith and, her mother, both of which, were starting to cause her real distress.

She needed to throw her focus on something far more light-hearted for a few days. And what better way to achieve that, than finding Nicholas.

He wasn't leaving for South Africa for another week, so she could try and find out from Rupert where he lived and could go and talk to him.

Cora thought she could surprise him. This would inevitably bring about two things: she would either make a complete fool of herself or, succeed in making Nicholas see, that running away from the one chance he had in a long time to love again, was madness.

Cora was dreaming the scene in her romantic imagination… Nicholas would swoop her up in his arms and tell her he had been a fool, and that it was too late to cancel his trip but wanted her to come with him. Life was too short surely not to allow herself to marvel about a happy future, in the arms of a lovely man… and the thought of all this made her feel instantly happier.

This was the side of Cora that was in many ways a little childish and naive. Not necessarily so with the expected immaturity of a young soul, but in a sense that was merely a beautifully simple way of looking at life, without any of the dreadful complications, that had afflicted her so often.

And why shouldn't she have a moment of totally romantic silliness, even if it did all go wrong.

She didn't have much to lose but there could be a lot to be gained from having the courage to approach Nicholas in this way. He would never expect this from her; he didn't know her well enough… Cora loved a surprise and this one, she thought, was a fabulous one.

It would distract her completely from what was going on at home, and serve as a real strengthening exercise.

Or so she hoped.

She rang Jill and asked for Rupert's mobile number, with the excuse that a friend of hers had been asked to write a piece for the paper on the new policies for shipping laws in Europe, and she had heard Rupert tell everyone, the evening of the dinner party, that he had great connections in that field.

This would keep Jill away from suspecting that her request could have anything to do with Nicholas.

Rupert was delighted to get Cora's message… she had decided to text him so to avoid having to explain exactly what it was she wanted from Nicholas, and Rupert hadn't asked, which Cora had appreciated.

In her text Cora just said that she might like to see him briefly before he left but hadn't absolutely decided on that, and could she please have his address or where he might be, for the next two or three days.

Rupert had been very quick at replying, which had helped to maintain Cora's momentum.

She was starting to feel the excitement of the surprise building fast inside her.

Nicholas was going to be in Ireland, at his cottage. That didn't exactly make it as easy as popping up to London for the evening, but Cora thought this was probably all meant to be.

Had it been an easy and fast place to get to, she wouldn't have spent the necessary time thinking about it first; because at least a little thinking, was needed for after all.

Even if she was to make a fool of herself, she might as well try and do it properly and with style.

She had lost a couple of pounds over the last week stressing about Raith and her mother which was all good as, although it seemed like so little weight off, it was part of those few pounds that just hang around her waist making her feel bloated and giving her neck an extra wrinkle which she hated. This would make her feel a little more confident. She looked at herself in the hall mirror and decided she could do with some highlights and she called her trusted hairdresser, Lydia, in Winchester, and begged her to squeeze her in, as soon as possible.

The hairdresser didn't really have the time, but Cora had been coming to her salon for many years and Lydia was very fond of her, so she promised to do something with her hair the next morning, as long as she could get in by 8 am.

If Cora was going to Ireland, she would need to stay the night somewhere, so she would research that, and then tried to find out a little more about the company Nicholas worked for.

Cora looked for pubs and nice B&Bs in the area. She would fly to Dublin, and then hire a car and by booking everything on-line, she could be ready to leave by tomorrow lunchtime. She called Sue before enquiring with the kennels, to see whether she could have Skye, again, and thankfully she was home and answered the phone straight away, and said she would love to. An hour later she had booked flights, car and her one-night stay in what looked like a lovely pub, only five minutes away from Nicholas's cottage.

The last booking might have been a bit rushed, as she suddenly thought that, if her surprise encounter with Nicholas didn't quite turn out as hoped, she would then be stuck for the night far too close to where he lived, and possibly, where he might have wanted to come to drown his sorrows after seeing her.

She was going all out with positive thinking, so there was no point making secondary plans to cover the 'if's'.

If she was going to crash, it might as well be a proper pile up and nothing as pathetic as a bicycle puncture!

Cora was driven by three forces over this plan: firstly, she wanted to find out about Nicholas's feelings towards her face to face, not just relying on what she had heard from Rupert, and understand his true reasons behind leaving for South Africa.

The second force pushing her forward was a therapeutic one; Cora needed to get herself out of the horrid cloud that had been hovering over her since Raith's letters, and going to Ireland, was putting all those worries at the very back of her mind and bringing forward, much happier feelings.

The third reason for doing this was the most forceful engine within her; Cora had spent her life trying her best to make people happy. This was what, ultimately, made her feel at her happiest too… to see happiness in others, especially if she could be the deliverer of such joy.

And for that moment, she was prepared to take this risk.

She was trying to imagine the look of surprise but also delight in Nicholas's face, when he would next see her. She hoped his eyes would, of course, be full of amusement and laughter.

The next day Cora drove to Gatwick, now and again checking herself in the small vanity mirror of the car. It always takes a while to get used to any style formulated in a hairdresser's, however lovely it may be, and this was no exception. Cora had opted for rather more highlights than she usually had, in the rush of the moment, and because she really couldn't quite make her mind up and felt like a little change.

The result had been a good one. Satisfactory enough anyway, and certainly in the sense that it gave her skin more light, nevertheless, she knew that it would take time to get used to it.

What she was sure of, was that her hair had been greatly improved from the second time Nicholas had seen her, when she had been caught taking her horrid woolly hat off in the pub!

At least it was beautifully smooth and shiny.

She kept her fingers crossed that the weather would hold, so not to ruin all this effort.

Cora was wearing lovely loose white linen trousers which would not look particularly clever in the middle of an Irish summer downpour, let alone as an accompaniment to her ghastly long-life companion: her woolly red hat which was always in her bag in case of rain.

The journey that followed was quite uneventful, apart from the woman sitting next to Cora, on the plane, who spent the whole flight coughing her heart out, and blowing her nose.

Why do people do that thought Cora, ungraciously, believing it to be OK to spread their germs all around? She wished she had brought her little pack of essential oils with her, so she could have had the opportunity to sniff a tissue full of tea tree and eucalyptus, but this trip was unlike any other.

None of it had been about taking intelligent preventative measures, as she usually did.

It was all about fate and spontaneous stupidity instead!

The road trip from the airport to the pub where she was staying, took far less time than expected and, to Cora's delight, the area, which was totally new to her, was outstandingly beautiful.

Cora, in fact, felt quite sad that she couldn't take far more time admiring the extraordinary landscape in front of her, which had seen her literally gasp a few times, in complete awe, since leaving Dublin.

She couldn't believe the splendour of the mountains, and the coast, on her way from Wicklow to Wexford, and all so soon after leaving the city. Now on her way towards Waterford, she longed to stop and go for a long walk with Skye, who would have loved it here.

If her trip turned out to be an utter disaster, she must at least remind herself to come back one day and discover this part of Ireland more fully.

Cora found the pub easily. It was quite small and tucked away in a very rural spot at the foot of a pretty hill. She settled in her room and freshened up, taking a few deep breaths and thinking aloud. What was she actually going to say to Nicholas, when she finally saw him?

She hadn't quite thought that through yet, but in many ways, Cora wanted to be genuinely honest with him about her reasons for coming, so the conversation may well turn out to be as much of a surprise to Nicholas, as it was to her.

She returned to the bar and asked the landlord just how long it would take her to get to Nicholas's cottage, as she had lost all reception on her mobile, and typically she hadn't thought of taking some notes down of the directions from here.

Apparently, it was only five minutes away and for some reason, the landlord, seemed particularly amused at her question, and threw his head backwards in laughter…

'Yes, the cottage is very close indeed, you can't miss it,' he said. Why he thought this was so funny, confused Cora, but he looked very red cheeked. She put it down to what he was probably drinking, under the counter.

She set off down a windy country lane, aware that she must be getting closer to the coast again, and came upon an enormous gate with a lodge.

Leaving the gate on her right, Cora carried on driving down the narrow lane, but eventually came to the end of it. There was only a large field ahead of her, with a combine harvester left in the middle of it, a job half done. She felt a little frustrated.

She must have been driving too fast, excited at being so close to her destination, and missed the turning for the cottage, so she did a 'U' turn and went back up towards the pub, at a much slower rate this time looking right and left of her, but couldn't find it.

The name he had given her was visibly carved on the stone pillar on the left of the entrance gate, *Cullen.*

Cora started envisaging a pretty little cottage with a view of the sea, but daydreaming wasn't going to get her there!

The pub where she had stayed the night before was called 'The Cullen Arms' and the lane she had taken from there was 'Cullen Lane', so it seemed that Cullen may just be the name of the area…

She wished the landlord could have been a little less focused on his tipple, and rather more precise in giving her the right directions to the cottage.

What a useless man.

Sometime between returning to the pub and setting off again, Cora's excitement and confidence started to abandon her.

She felt a little bit scared and panicked, her old anxieties rushing up her throat, and thought that maybe she should turn around and drive home, now, before making a complete fool of herself.

She was still in time to do that.

And, it would be absolutely fine, she told herself. After all, nobody at home knew where she was, and nobody here knew her.

She suddenly felt very hot… a hot flush coming on just when she didn't need one, but it took her mind off panicking.

Cora slowed right down and waited for it to go.

By this point she was awkwardly parked on the verge of the lane, just before the lodge. She longed to see a sign for Cullen Cottage, to give her hope that she was on the right track. She needed a little boost, both geographically and psychologically.

She decided to head through the main gates, and then ask the first person she came across for help; the drive seemed to wind on and on. It was all beautifully kept but something about it was changing; she started noticing recently mowed grass either side of the road which surely meant she must be getting closer to a destination. Not Nicholas's obviously as the gate and lodge indicated that she was driving towards a country house of some importance and size, but at least somewhere she could enquire about Nicholas's house.

The drive had been rather windy and hardwoods were shading both sides of the road; Cora had now driven for about a mile and suddenly the lane seemed to open up into an extraordinary expanse of open land on either side with the most enormous house at the very end of it.

That must be Cullen House, she thought, and it was still at least a quarter of a mile off; she couldn't see it in great detail, but it certainly looked incredibly elegant. As she approached it, she couldn't see any cars parked in front of it but maybe they entered the house from the back and parked there.

She would stop here and ask for directions.

She could have done with going to the loo, after the hassle of not finding her way as quickly as expected, and, arriving there within the planned five minutes from the pub, but that may be pushing her luck.

Cora would have to start the process all over again, take a deep breath, reapply her lip-gloss, check her hair for the third time at least since leaving the pub (!) and, with a bit more positive thinking this time, forget all the mishaps about not finding her way first time round.

The front door, which was huge and wooden, had one of those old-fashioned brass bells, that you pull at, very hard, and then let go of.

She did this a couple of times although she couldn't tell whether her efforts were producing any noise at all. She tried a third, then forth time but nobody came.

'Arghhh... ', Cora uttered.

Her mobile was still showing no reception at all, so the only thing left to do was to drive back from where she came from, and ask someone who looked better informed in the pub. She couldn't believe Nicholas lived five minutes from the Cullen Arms and she couldn't find the blasted place.

'Calm down', Cora told her herself, 'you have come all the way from Hampshire to surprise someone so no point getting in a state just because you can't work out the last five minutes of the journey.'

She took a couple of very deep breaths and closed her eyes. She hadn't forgotten that she always kept a little bottle of geranium oil with her in her bag, and she poured a couple of drops on to the left cuff of her cardigan, and inhaled, deeply.

This always had an immediate calming effect on Cora.

After a few minutes she felt re-energised, and she was ready to go and feeling much better.

She started the car and, as she reversed, she noticed in her back mirror someone walking towards her from the back of the house.

'Yes!' she exclaimed, someone had heard her at last.

Cora dashed out of her car with a mixture of relief and frustration and suddenly realised the person facing her was Nicholas.

14

Cora didn't have the time to think of why he was here and not at his cottage.

Nicholas stopped in his tracks as soon as he recognised her, and just stared at her as if he had seen a ghost.

Oh my god, Cora thought… He is horrified I am here.

She wanted to be swallowed away by the earth beneath her.

Nicholas must have had no idea she had spoken to Rupert about all his plans.

Cora realised, quite suddenly, that she must have been mad to have thought this was going to be exciting… it was more like a nightmare.

While all this was going through her head, only two seconds had passed of course if not less, but it felt like five minutes.

Cora couldn't have been more wrong about her assumptions. Before she could open her mouth to speak, Nicholas had started walking again towards her with a huge smile on his face, and he was now laughing.

'How lovely to see you Cora, although rather unexpected, are you in Ireland on holiday?', he said.

This time it was Cora who laughed. Too loudly probably but the relief she felt in that instant, was nothing but overwhelming.

She couldn't quite think how much of the truth she wanted to let go of right now, as she was cherishing this moment so much. She had forgotten how handsome Nicholas was.

Cora's heart was beating so fast that she could actually hear it; she hoped Nicholas couldn't guess her state of mind.

He was wearing, what looked like, a very old and probably loved jumper, with more than a few holes in it, and gardening gloves.

Was he doing some odd jobs for the people who lived in the house?

She told him that she had nearly given up on finding his cottage, and how the landlord at the Cullen Arms had laughed when giving her directions, which had proven to be both unhelpful and rather useless.

Nicholas was enjoying this!

He could just imagine what must have gone through Michael's head at the pub, while trying to help Cora find her way.

He was not in the habit of letting people know where he lived, unless they were very close friends.

Nicholas had inherited Cullen from his parents, but had not spent much time here since they had died so every visit was a very busy one, dealing with estate matters, the rented cottages, the wall garden, the park, the shoot and the farms, although the latter were let out now, leaving very little time for Nicholas to use the house for entertaining.

His life at Cullen was a private one. He was a humble person and he so often came across people, in his charitable work, who were in such severe poverty, that coming here felt a little peculiar at times.

Nicholas appreciated immensely how lucky he was to own such a beautiful place, and wanted to do everything he could, to keep it so. He was blessed with the most wonderful estate manager, Peter Hall, who had been with him for ten years now, and knew he could trust him completely. This was another factor that had made it possible for him to go to Africa. The house was far too big for one person, but Nicholas loved it and he didn't have the heart to sell it, as it had been in his family for generations. For two weeks in August and at Christmas time, all Nicholas's extended family still gathered here, as they had done for many years, and the house truly came alive.

Cora was enjoying finding out a bit more about Nicholas's life in Ireland.

She decided to come clean about her coffee with Rupert, explaining that their meeting had been a complete coincidence, and that Rupert had mentioned that Nicholas, was going to leave for Africa very soon.

She also admitted to him, that this was one of the reasons she had decided to come over for a day or so, also adding that the other reason was that she had been dying to visit Ireland for years, and had decided to kill two birds with one stone.

Nicholas wasn't a fool and could tell that there was more to this than Cora was prepared to say, but left it at that.

He was genuinely so delighted to see her, that he didn't want to spoil the moment by asking her too many questions.

The only one he did ask her, was whether she was free for supper, and whether she would like to spend the evening with him, considering the effort she had made to get here.

The awkwardness that had been born after their last meeting, faded away quickly, leaving a distinctly flirtatious atmosphere which they were both enjoying.

Nicholas decided it was only fair to show Cora his house, so he suggested she got back into her car while he went to the back of Cullen House to pick up his own, so that she could follow him.

There was no reason for Cora to have suspected in any way that this was in fact Nicholas's home, as he had described a cottage to Cora; the house where his mother had lived, before dying and leaving it to him. There had been some truth in that as his mother had indeed moved into one of the cottages on the estate, after his father had died, but Nicholas had never lived there himself.

Nicholas drove past Cora and she followed. They disappeared down the long straight drive and, just before continuing along the road she had driven down half an hour beforehand, he turned right down a rough track which she had noticed, but hadn't taken, as it had no signs to indicate where it was going to.

She now wished she hadn't been so stressed and had tried it earlier, rather than nearly giving up and deciding that the only solution was to return to the pub.

Nicholas must have thought she was rather dumb not to have taken this route and gone all the way to the main house. She was longing to discover the sweet cottage his mother had lived in, and imagined it having a small rose garden and some lovely herbs, by the kitchen door.

But Nicholas seemed to be driving into a large yard, which backed onto what looked like, the back of a very large house, and then through an arch and out again, onto the other side only to find herself exactly where she had parked five minutes before!

He got out of his car and opened her door, welcoming her with open arms to his humble abode and then started laughing so much that his eyes started tearing.

'Is this truly your home Nicholas?' asked Cora, 'you told me that your mother had died leaving you a lovely small cottage?'

'That was partly true', he said. 'The cottage is here, on the estate and close to the coast, it's in a beautiful spot.'

Nicholas gave Cora a hug and asked her to forgive him for not telling her the full story, but when they had first met, he had never expected her to ever visit Cullen. He took her round the house which was beautiful and the view of the sea from the other side, from what was the back of it, was breathtaking. What an incredible place to have grown up in, Cora thought.

She suspected nothing inside the house had changed much for quite a few years, although the kitchen was spectacular, and very contemporary in style.

Nicholas told her that he had commissioned a very well-known Irish architect, who specialised in renovating large country houses, to design it. The architect had been brilliant at managing to merge old with new in an effortless and magical way.

Cora thought for an instant of her father and his work and how he would have loved to have seen the property and what Nicholas had done with it.

Her mind turned towards her mother for an instant as, she too, had a very good eye for interiors and would appreciate the beauty and design of this wonderful place, but soon shook that thought away as it didn't make her feel particularly happy.

The kitchen was made up of three areas, each of which flowed cleverly into the next…

The working side had a large green Aga, and a huge marble

top island; there was a dining area with a big oak table with a bench on one side and five chairs on the other, and, closest to a large bay window, overlooking the sea, were two large blue sofas with a TV.

The colours of the walls, as well as the sofa material and all the cushions, including the square ones by the kitchen table, were all pastel, and looked gentle, inviting and relaxing; pale blues, a very soft yellow, and a subtle washed out green.

Nicholas had very good taste; this pleased Cora. She always noticed house interiors and felt they often reflected the character of the person living in them.

However, Cullen gave off an air of such calm and peace that it seemed a bit of a contradiction to the Nicholas she had got to know a little, and certainly, not the impression she had had from Rupert of what was going on in his dear friend's head or, his life in general.

The man Cora had fallen for at Jill's dinner party, was one not at all at peace with himself.

May be that is why he loved this place so much... because it reminded him of his youth, and it was where he could block out the rest.

Cora wondered how much of Cullen reminded Nicholas of his family?

She suspected Sandra would never have set foot in this place and, as Nicholas had never married, no significant other would have put a stamp on the house. As far as Cora was aware, Selina and her family had never visited either.

For no fault of his, Nicholas had never had a chance to bring his daughter here, or his grandchildren.

Cora's gut feelings about this lovely man's life here, was partly correct.

Nicholas did love spending time in Ireland although it was never enough and suggested that it allowed him to live in the past in some ways, but not in an unhappy way.

He truly cherished it and worked hard to make sure the estate could sustain itself, without costing him a fortune. In the last ten years, they had taken back in hand the smallest farm and, had diversified to raise more income, so that they could secure a safe future for Cullen as it stood. It had a children's farm which many of the local schools visited regularly, where they encouraged a lot of hands on management of the animals, from chickens to pigs.

They had set up a great farm shop and they were in the process of creating a mountain bike track, a fantastic high rope course, a zip wire and a climbing wall so the estate certainly didn't stand still.

All of which was about three miles away, and that was as much diversifying as Nicholas was intending to do. Many friends had suggested to him that the obvious source of income for a grand house like Cullen with such a stunning park, would have been to hold events, weddings and maybe have a conference centre. However, that was not a direction he was willing to take; not yet, at least.

If he could afford it, he wanted to avoid having people in the house and the grounds immediately surrounding it.

'But enough about this place, Cora. You must tell me, what really brought you to this end of Ireland and in fact, to Ireland at all?', he asked.

Oh dear thought Cora, she had tried to say but he obviously hadn't taken it in… he really had no idea, and she suddenly feared he might be horrified to learn that she had made the journey all the way from home, to come and see him, and him alone, before he left. She was sure she had tried to tell him earlier, but he must have thought she was flirting and joking around, to make him laugh.

Cora left too long a gap for it to feel comfortable, she didn't have the time to think what she wanted to say, whether the truth, or half, or not at all. She could, of course, just be visiting a friend or relation etc. They had been chatting for what seemed like ages about the house and the estate and all that was going on here at Cullen, and he had caught her completely off guard.

She felt hot and thought she might faint all of a sudden out of fear that he might think her simply mad to have acted so impulsively. Cora took a few deep breaths and a long sip of her wine and spoke gently but with intent, looking straight into his eyes.

'Nicholas, I meant what I said before and yes, I did make the journey from home to see you. I felt sad to hear from Rupert that you had decided to leave and go to Africa for a while and I wasn't sure whether your decision may have been brought on by anything I might have said to you, when we were last together. I felt, I needed to know. Please forgive me for suddenly turning up here, completely unannounced.'

Cora took another deep breath as she could see that he wasn't going to respond yet and so added, 'I felt we had such a great connection and I felt, may be wrongly, that part of you was really enjoying my company and wanted more, but on the other hand, something about you also wanted to run away.'

'I wasn't sure what you were running from and I know you tried to explain it to me briefly, but you also brought our conversation to an end rather abruptly., without letting me have a chance to reply or tell you my thoughts.'

Cora was trying to read his facial expression, but couldn't even start to guess his thoughts from the way he was watching her.

She felt as if she was rehearsing in front of a director who was interviewing for a part in a play…

'I felt the need to understand something which had been left wide open, open to confusion mainly, before you left. I am not very good at letting go until things are resolved and I appreciate nothing had happened between us at all, but I still felt very sad about it because I like you, very much,' said Cora.

Nicholas looked deeply into her eyes while she was saying all this and never looked away. She could tell that he was taking it all in and that he was probably thinking that this time, it would be harder to run away from her as she was, after all, sitting in his house, so he may have to expose himself rather more, and be a little more honest towards her than he had wished.

Whether she was going to like what he had to say was another question of course, but Cora had pushed the issue this far, so she may as well go even further.

She had made a bloody long journey to come and speak to him, so there was no point leaving too many stones unturned.

Cora had had the impression from Nicholas, during their first meeting, that he would never be the kind of person one knows everything about. There would probably, always be a side to him, albeit small, that would remain mysterious.

Nicholas suddenly got up from the sofa in the kitchen which they had shared until that moment, and started walking towards the door… Cora feared she must have said too much.

He can't have been used to this kind of very open and honest way of talking that she had just put him through… not many men would have been, in fact.

Nicholas opened the door and disappeared leaving her sitting there not quite knowing what to do next, but within a couple of minutes, just as Cora was starting to wonder whether it may be best for her to make an exit, and return to the safety of the pub, he came back holding what looked like a very large green book.

It was an old photograph album.

15

Nicholas sat next to her and just said 'I would like to show you my family.'

He gently started turning the pages of what was his life story in the beautiful, leather bound album.

Cora watched silently, while Nicholas, talked her through the pictures, many of which showed a child, sitting on the steps by the front door of this house, or in the grounds of Cullen, often appearing with a dog.

Later Cora learnt that the dog, Spice, had had a very important place in Nicholas's life, and one that had made his returns from school, near London, and back to Ireland, particularly joyous occasions.

There were photos of Selina, as a baby, ones which Nicholas had had to beg Sandra for, and although there were only a few of them, they represented enough for Nicholas to cherish. He had taken as many as he could too, every year, when he was with them, in Australia.

So many in fact, that it was hard to imagine that Nicholas's daughter and family, didn't live close by.

The sadness of course was that Selina's smile captured often by Nicholas in the shots, belonged to a woman so loved by him, but one of course, who was totally unaware of his true identity.

Nicholas explained that because Sandra's husband had adopted Selina when she was just a baby, he had never been able to tell her that he was her father, and still hadn't to this day, so his relationship was not altogether a happy one, as he couldn't ever be completely himself with her.

And by consequence, he couldn't tell the children he was their grandfather or, expect and hope for a more intimate relationship, which would have no doubt entailed phone calls and photographs sent back and forwards throughout the whole year, and regular visits from them to Cullen.

Cora noticed that some of the photographs included Ray, Sandra's husband, and asked Nicholas why this was.

'I have to include him in some of them too, so as not to look strange, but I dislike Ray,' he said.

'Not because he is Sandra's husband or due to jealousy, but because Ray has always made a point of putting me down, and I know you will think this is rather pathetic of me, that I should just ignore him, but I don't find it easy', he said.

It had apparently become rather a joke which Sandra seemed to go along with, probably to please Ray and make him feel reassured. So, although all this took place for only a few days of the year, Cora was starting to understand what a huge impact this had on Nicholas's mind and soul every time he was there.

And not only when he was there…

Cora felt such sympathy for the man sitting next to her.

She loved the fact that he cared so much for his daughter, and her family, and she respected and admired his sense of duty towards them and his incredible resilience, considering the manner in which he had to go along with Sandra wishes.

But Cora was also beginning to sense that, had Nicholas been able to let go of the guilt of having fathered a child, who had been taken such a long way away and, whose mother would have much preferred no contact with him at all, his life may well have turned out to be very different.

She suspected that Selina had been the main reason Nicholas had been reluctant to marry, and have another family, feeling that he had made such a mess first time round.

Cora wondered whether his yearly visits to Australia, served more as a renewed guilt trip and a self-confidence stripping exercise, than much else.

She was probably being rather harsh, in her judgement, but she couldn't bear to watch this lovely man, torture himself, in this way.

Nicholas had told Cora during their last encounter, that he had also felt unable to provide the commitment most women would like, because of his job, which entailed a huge amount of travelling.

Ultimately, he was now resigned to working hard for the business which he loved and co-owned and, maintaining Cullen in the best possible shape he could.

Nicholas admitted to Cora that every time he came back to Cullen, he would spend hours, sitting just where they were now, looking at this album. Cora couldn't imagine being in the same situation and her thoughts went to her own children and she suddenly felt so blessed, in so many ways.

She looked at Nicholas, at his gentle eyes; was it kindness she could see in them, or was it grief ?

His situation must have weighed on him hugely, and he spoke about it with sadness, but also, a brave and resigned reality.

Cora couldn't help feeling the waste.

Waste of such precious times in his life, lost because Nicholas had basically chosen to eliminate any chance of deep affection, love and intimacy, because of a 'mistake' made when he was very young and was fearful that this may lead to making another. She viewed it, nearly, as a kind of self-inflicted punishment, in fact she felt convinced that he viewed his choice of life as such.

How could he keep viewing Selina as a mistake? He had used that word with her several times to describe that night with Sandra in Bali.

'A terrible mistake' had been his choice of words. 'One I must pay for' he had said.

Cora decided to speak up about her feelings.

'Nicholas, I do understand why you are feeling like this, but I also feel sad that you describe the consequences of your first encounter with Sandra when you were travelling, as a 'mistake'.'

'Of course the circumstances were hardly ideal, and will never be, because you live so far away from Selina, and she didn't come into this world, through a conventional union. But can't you see what a wonderful person you have helped create and bring into this world? said Cora.

'Can't you stop viewing this in such a negative way and try and be grateful that you have a daughter, and that she is alive and well and whether Sandra likes it or not, she is half of you?

Nicholas didn't say a word, he seemed to be waiting for Cora to carry on with her diagnosis and opinions.

Whether this was a good thing or a bad omen, Cora couldn't be too sure, but she had started so she felt she may as well finish what she wished to say to him.

'Many people spend their lives wanting children and can't, some die young before they can, and some have children who don't survive past the age of five. There is so much to be grateful for having Selina in your life, even in the way that it has to be.'

'You could have married, and had more children, and most women would have accepted and understood the situation with Sandra, especially as it only involves you being away for one week of the year, at the most,' carried on Cora.

'I could just imagine Cullen filled with happy family life, children's voices and teenagers and you enjoying being part of all that. How it must have been when you were a child. This is such a wonderfully dreamy place Nicholas, but it doesn't feel truly alive; I am sorry if I am so bold in saying this… but I worry, from what you have told me today, that Cullen has just become where you hide from the world'.

Nicholas had still not moved or whispered a word.

Cora chose to carry on, 'I understand that your present situation, in many ways, does bring you contentment but does it make you deeply happy, or are you purely living a life of guilt with regards to Selina, and duty towards your parents and the estate?'

Cora felt she had now said all she wished.

She probably had, in fact, gone too far in her boldness and honesty, but she had always taken the option of speaking her mind, whenever life called for it, rather than the more British way of silently keeping it in and moving on.

She didn't feel she had much to lose, as nothing had truly started between them, so this would either be the icing on the cake, or it would put Nicholas off her altogether. Maybe he would never come back from Africa at all! Or it maybe enough to make him think hard about his past choices and wake up to the opportunity that might lie ahead of him now.

The ball was very clearly in his court, and Cora quietly waited for his reaction.

But there was none from Nicholas at all.

Nicholas did not reply, or comment on anything Cora had said.

She thought this a most extraordinary way of spending an evening.

Nicholas got up and offered Cora another drink, and then quietly started cooking a simple but delicious supper of venison and lovely fresh vegetables from his garden.

He talked about many things, but never touching on his life again, his imminent choices, his past, or plans for the future.

He spent most of the evening asking her about herself and her family and especially about Francis, Belle and Ludo.

At about eleven o'clock, Cora felt this seemed the natural moment to take her leave.

The fact that Nicholas had not spoken to her about the thoughts and questions she had put to him, was obviously a clear sign that those were subjects he was not prepared to be questioned on, and although he seemed very friendly and appeared to enjoy her company, she felt this was the end of the road.

Cora wasn't going to view coming all the way here as a waste. She was determined to see the positive sides of the visit. She had seen a part of Ireland that was utterly beautiful and new to her.

She had come here to Cullen, which was obviously a very special place, and had enjoyed listening to Nicholas's ideas for the estate and his determination to keep it going.

'Yes, it had not really been bad at all… a couple of days away from home after all,' thought Cora aloud.

What Cora was doing in fact was trying to 'lessen-the- blow', not allowing the disappointment to show on her face in front of Nicholas, or in her heart, for her own good and self-protection.

In her defence, at least she had tried her best, although her way of trying her best was not necessarily everyone's. Cora had been very direct and forward but, at the end of the day, that was who she was, and time was of the essence as he was just about to leave for another continent.

If he couldn't cope with that, there was really no point pretending that they could form any sort of relationship. One thing she was not prepared to do, was to wait for someone to decide whether he liked her enough, after six months in isolation in Africa, while trying to find himself.

Cora had had her fair share of men needing to find themselves, and from the latest revelations, it seemed that her potential father may have been one of them too… although what Raith Browne suffered from most, was finding himself regularly in the wrong bed.

Strangely, Cora felt a new energy about her this morning, as she awoke in the heavily decorated room in the pub. Something strong inside her, told her that she needed to return home. And not as a loser, but as a winner.

She had turned the corner and had not allowed her sympathy and compassion, for once, to steer her towards nursing Nicholas or, mothering him. She had instead walked away from him, his issues and insecurities. This was very much against her character and she could see, vividly, that it had been an unusual reaction for her. It was nevertheless a very positive one.

Last night, she had of course felt those old vibes of longing to be with him, to stay the night, had he wished for that, and get deeply involved, had he wished for that too. But now she was proud for leaving with her head held high, and about to plan her return back to Hampshire. She missed Skye's wise eyes and damp nose on her lap; the security of the cottage.

She paid her bill at the bar and made her way back, taking a slightly different route this time, and making a stop in Narragmore to grab a bite. She would come back one day, and bring Skye and return to the coastal road, and stop and take her for lovely walks on the beach.

By the time Cora arrived home, it was ten in the evening. She didn't feel particularly tired, so she decided to have a glass of wine and check her emails and post. Although she had only left yesterday, it felt, strangely, like far longer than that.

She looked different somehow, and it took her a few seconds to notice that this was mainly due to the fact that her hair had changed; her trip to the hairdresser, the previous day, had been so last minute, that she had practically forgotten about it.

Again, she looked upon her spontaneous and rather sudden visit to Ireland, as something good.

Cora, felt that she knew and understood Nicholas a little better now, and she really liked him, even though they were not matched well romantically. She had wished him an interesting and fulfilling time in Africa. He was a good man and, in many ways, ticked so many boxes in what was Cora's imaginary list of potential companions, but he had been, and remained, terribly hard on himself.

And she could not and would not, alter his attitude towards his past, or be able to make him happy, when all he really felt was punishment and duty.

That could be someone else's job.

16

Cora slept badly for a few days after her return from Cullen. She had a niggling pain in her back, which she had felt about a month before. It had nearly disappeared altogether, allowing her to feel that it didn't need attention, but she felt uncomfortable again.

She decided to give herself till the weekend and then, if no better, she would make an appointment with Charlie Granger, her osteopath.

Cora knew Charlie very well and enjoyed going to him, not only because he was able to fix her sore muscles, but because he was of great reassurance to her.

She had been visiting his practice for twenty years, as she often suffered a sore neck, caused by a car crash in her early twenties, and it was a bit like visiting a close friend. Charlie was so easy to talk to, but in some ways that was exactly the reason Cora had put off booking an appointment this time.

When she last saw Charlie a couple of months ago, she had burst into tears in front of him and later felt so pathetic and embarrassed. Charlie had been so caring and protective of Cora, probably, because he felt that she wasn't always good at putting herself first.

He knew what a kind person she was, and how much of her time was spent looking after other people, which, at times and inevitably, left her feeling emotionally very drained.

He was also aware that Cora suffered from anxiety, and how debilitating this had become for her in the past.

Since Cora's father's sudden death from cancer, her health concerns had escalated, to the point that she would often ask Charlie his advice to help her calm down, and they would end up spending the first half of the session in his practice, talking about her worries, and the other half, being treated by him for her back and neck.

So, going to Charlie's, was far more than just a visit to an osteopath. He had always been wonderfully kind to Cora, although a little surprised to see her in such a state of mind, as she had spent nearly a year on her own already, and he had sincerely hoped, she had been growing stronger every day.

What Cora had failed to notice for all these years was, that Charlie, was more than a little fond of her, and would do anything to see her feeling happy.

He had suffered badly at the end of a long-term relationship, many years before, and he had put serious liaisons at the bottom of his priority list.

Cora suspected that Charlie now felt most at ease by being in total control of his emotional state, and she believed that he viewed the only way to achieve this, was to be on his own.

This had jolted him into a passion for extreme fitness and he had competed in the 'Ironman' a handful of times, and regularly took part in triathlons, which, Cora felt, was probably his way of coping with life on his own, and keeping his mind fully occupied when he wasn't over the treatment table.

Charlie had never made a pass at her and never felt he should, also because he was certain that Cora, although fond of him, didn't feel the same.

So whenever Cora booked an appointment, Charlie did all he could to nurse, not only her physical complaints, but reassure her mind from whatever was troubling her, reminding her of what a wonderful person she was; he would tell her that the problem with her life, was simply that she just hadn't come across anyone decent enough to realise that.

Every time he said that, it made Cora laugh out loud and it had become their parting joke.

The energy, and strength, Cora had felt on waking up in the pub in Ireland that morning, seemed to have drained out of her.

Returning home had initially given her that cosy, and secure feeling she cherished, especially after her exchanges with Nicholas, but she felt herself wondering about her childhood again. Her thoughts returned to Raith and wondering whether he was her father.

Cora had suffered from depression twice in the past, a long time ago now, but she remembered finding huge comfort in self-help books and poetry, and was very knowledgeable about which alternative medicines could help in those situations. She knew that when strength of mind was a must, she needed to be proactive, and find it, deep within herself, to use these methods.

She reminded herself of the rules she had made and written down, to help her relax, sleep and meditate, so she went in search of a file she had put together.

Sleep was her number one necessity and she hadn't had much of that lately or, at least, not quality sleep. She could blame hot flushes for that, but she also knew that if she gave herself a couple of hours in the afternoon to catch up, she would be far better off. And the wonderful thing was that, unlike most people who worked away from their homes, she was in a position where an afternoon nap, was not unfeasible.

Cora thought that secondly, she must fill her time with as many things to do as possible and ideally, not things which involved her being alone.

This of course was easier said than done as her job was a lonely one, but she had been thinking of increasing her time spent on it.

Cora had been waiting for the paper to come back to her, with a reply to her request of producing a second weekly article for them.

Politics had been as frustrating as it had been gripping, since the Brexit vote, and she would have loved to get more involved in the commentary of the moment.

There was so much happening in government, that she hadn't felt altogether satisfied with her writing lately.

In fact Cora was starting to feel that whatever she ended up writing about, was sounding a bit like old news, as events seemed to change so incredibly quickly, so it was becoming increasingly hard to produce an article that felt original and fresh, by the time it came to print.

She had also, so often, promised herself she must try and get more involved with her community, whether this meant doing some evening classes or helping in the village charity shop, or learning yoga.

Anything that would involve interaction with other human beings, and therefore, would give her mind a break from wondering off in the wrong direction.

All she needed were people. People she could talk to, anyone as well as Skye.

Cora was intelligent, and she enjoyed sharing thoughts and opinions with people who were stimulated by challenging and rousing subjects of conversation, not by inconsequential tittle-tattle. She had no time for gossip.

She was also becoming more and more aware that all this business with Raith and her mother, was not only getting her down, but was occupying a huge chunk of her mind. It was delving into a past that did little more than emphasise further the differences between Belinda, and herself.

But Cora still yearned to find out the truth, mainly because it would finally provide her with a reason why Belinda felt the way she did towards her. She recognised that it was becoming like a brick wall in her mind, one that was stopping her from moving on.

By the time she had started her breakfast, Cora was remembering all sorts of encounters with her mother, especially over the last few years. She was trying to play back their conversations and her general attitude, in what had sadly become a very strained relationship between them.

Cora made a promise to herself; from tomorrow morning she would start running again and she would do so first thing.

She knew how helpful this had proven in the past and she was so determined not to allow herself to slip back into feeling depressed.

Within a week, not thinking about her visit to Ireland and Nicholas, had become far easier than she expected.

She felt this was rather intriguing as she had liked him very much, but this may be down to the fact that she was growing older, and wiser, and there was no point crying over spilled milk, or feeling too upset about someone who was leaving for a different continent in a few days.

Nicholas was definitely on the 'back burner' for now, she felt with relief.

The next day as Cora opened her front door ready for another run, she looked up at the sky; it was a dull, dark grey. It was pouring down. But this was not going to stop her, in fact it made her even more determined to run faster. She returned 30 minutes later with a very clear mind.

She would shower and dress smartly, then drive over to Belinda's and have it all out. This time, she told herself, she would not come home until she had confronted her mother.

Today, she would wait all day by Belinda's front door, if she had to. She wasn't sure that she was necessarily prepared for any consequences this may lead to, but she had to do it. Had to resolve it in her head.

If Belinda decided never to speak to her again, she would have to except that. It would hardly make much of a difference to their relationship after all. As Cora parked her car in front of her mother's house, she was relieved to see that she was in. Belinda's own car was parked in the garage, which she often left open. She hadn't, in any way, prepared what she was going to say, as she decided this would make her feel scared and nervous... she would just come out and say it, somehow.

She pressed the bell rather than walking in, wanting to give herself a little extra time, and waited, taking in a deep breath and then another and, as the wait was longer than expected, she took another, fearing that her mother may have been on the phone or in the bathroom.

If her mother was in, Cora could just imagine how the noise of the bell ringing numerous times, would irritate her.

She rang once more but then started to worry. Could she have fallen?

She mustn't panic. Belinda had probably walked into the village for something.

She tried her mobile, but it was switched off, as so often was the case.

She felt that breaking a window at this point may be over reacting and, if she did so, and her mother turned out to be shopping, she would be furious with her, so Cora returned to her car and decided to wait for an hour, and then make a decision.

Half an hour later, the roar of a car arriving at the house made her slip down into her seat so quickly that she hit her head on the steering wheel.

She recognised the noise and she remained paralysed in that position, realising that pulling herself back up would look so stupid now, but neither could she think of how she was going to get herself out of this tight spot.

Silence followed the halting of the car, so she didn't think anyone had stepped out of it yet.

It had to be Raith, she knew that noise but what she didn't know yet, was whether he had seen her.

As she started moving slowly upwards, she heard her mother's voice and the closing of the heavy door of the E-type.

The car started off and left.

This was so embarrassing thought Cora but at least it had saved her from wondering how to approach the subject of Raith. She couldn't believe that he had told her that he returned to Hampshire to make a new start with Helena, but in reality, was already seeing Belinda again.

Cora now felt an even stronger urge to find out what was going on.

She felt angry and betrayed by a man she hardly knew.

She looked up to see her mother peeking into the car looking straight at her.

'What are you doing?' said Belinda.

'I came to see you,' replied Cora.

'I can see that, so you'd better come in.'

Cora pulled herself out from the awkward position she had pushed herself in and followed her mother into the house.

They sat in the kitchen and Belinda sat opposite her and waited for Cora to speak.

This was not exactly the plan Cora had in mind. She felt like a silly girl, who had been caught doing something naughty, and was getting a telling off from her teacher.

She had hoped to start her conversation from quite a different platform… but too late for that now, and no easy way to recover from where she found herself. She must make a start with what she had come for, before losing what little courage was left.

Cora thought she might as well start from the beginning and told her mother about Jill's accident the day she had been asked to go for dinner. She was explaining that she had tried to get to the house early, to be there to welcome Jill's guests, when her mobile started ringing.

Cora searched for it in her handbag, somewhat irritated by the noise as she felt that she had found a good flow in conversation, and just wanted to get to the point now, as soon as possible, before losing her nerve.

She felt her mobile at the bottom of her bag, and was about

to turn it onto silent mode, but something deep inside her told her she should answer. Of course, at this point Belinda still had no idea that Cora had met Raith, let alone that she was aware of their past… or had she?

Nothing could ever have prepared Cora for what happened next.

17

Belinda was sitting on the opposite side of her kitchen island when her daughter took the call, and was hoping this wouldn't take long as she had things she wanted to get on with. Suddenly, she noticed, something was wrong. Cora had a sense of having turned white, and was just answering in monosyllables. Belinda drew a short breath and stretched her hand to grab the side of her stool…

'What's happened?' asked Belinda.

'Darling, what it is?' she asked again, this time moving towards her daughter, fearing she may fall to the floor.

'It's Belle. She was in an accident on her way to work.'

'She's gone, mum, she is dead,' whispered Cora, and let herself slide off the stool.

The two women held each other tightly, like they had never done before, and Cora felt her whole world collapse around her.

She felt freezing cold, violently sick and lightheaded.

Belinda just held on to her, without saying a word.

How could this be… how can a child be taken from her mother in such a sudden way, that allows for no preparation, causing such profound devastation that nothing on earth can be equal to it.

The pain Cora was feeling right now was so immense, that she just wanted to be swallowed up, she wanted to die with her Belle, if this meant being close to her again.

Could she block this horrific moment from her mind for a few seconds… close her eyes and pretend it had just been a nightmare?

She must let Francis and Ludo know… she hadn't even asked Mark whether he had called them already.

She felt overwhelmed by a tsunami of emotions, flash backs, memories, desperate fears of what may have been Belle's last moments, possibly in great pain. Cora's practical side, had completely abandoned her.

She couldn't bear the thought, that her darling daughter, might have suffered terrible pain, before dying. She hadn't been there for her; when she needed her most. She had not been able to hold her, to tell her how much she loved her, and that she was going to be alright.

Belinda tried to lift her up, hoping to help her to the sofa, but Cora's body was just rigid.

Then suddenly Belinda sat down and broke into a desperate wail, followed by uncontrollable tears.

This brought Cora back into the present, and she stared at her mother, not knowing what to do with herself, let alone how to reach out to her.

So many years had passed for these two women during which lies, and emotional distance, had been chosen over honesty and genuine love. The holding back of their true feelings, had caused the slow inevitable rising of a wall, if not always between them, certainly running alongside them.

This morning, with the shock of Belle's death, Cora and Belinda had been violently thrown together into unknown territory; if a stranger had entered Belinda's kitchen now, he would have been forgiven for thinking they had been in an awful fight as they were both sitting at opposite sides of the room, just like animals, seemingly licking their wounds, not daring to move towards each other.

It was an inexplicable scene; one of horrendous sorrow.

A few minutes passed without either saying a word and then Cora stood up and went to her mother.

She hugged her and held her, and they lay on the sofa like that for what seemed like an eternity.

Belinda felt her daughter's despair, as her head lay on her chest, and she felt an overwhelming amount of love for her.

Why had she waited so long to allow this affection between them, to creep back into their lives?

Why had she waited for such a tragedy to make them close again?

Belinda felt full of remorse.

She had shown such a hard exterior to Cora for so many years, after feeling the unbearable hurt of losing Raith. And the reason for their break-up, had been mostly driven by the death of his eldest son. She suddenly understood his pain.

For the first time, Belinda felt she understood Raith's and Helena's despair, now, as she stared at her own daughter's utter anguish.

In these first moments of total bewilderment and emotional trauma, Belinda knew one thing with absolute certainty; she would completely and utterly forgive the man she had loved for most of her life, as her own selfishness now stood staring at her in horror. She felt more than that, she now respected and admired him for his strength.

The anger and resentment she had felt inside for both Raith and Cora for so long, anger that would inevitably be very complex to explain, let alone justify, had slipped away with Belle's death.

But for now, it was all about trying to get through today, and then the next day, and the next; somehow.

It had been nearly an hour since the news and Mark had called again to say he was driving to London to tell Francis and Ludo, and then he intended to drive back to Cora's house as he felt they should be together there tonight.

This news was hard enough to accept, without the practicalities of where Mark was going to sleep.

Then the reality of what had happened hit her again, and that, of course, Belle's bedroom would not be used,... would never again be slept in by their daughter.

Ever.

Cora wasn't sure of whether she wished to know more about Belle's death, or not.

She had not asked Mark, and he had simply said that it had been a car accident. Cora had been far too frightened to ask for more information. She feared desperately that, as Mark had not said that Belle had died instantly, she probably had suffered, in which case, Cora wasn't sure she could quite cope with that knowledge.

Not yet anyway.

Not today.

Maybe never.

But the thought wouldn't leave her mind...

Had she died instantly, or had she been seriously injured and then, maybe, she had died in the ambulance, or soon after reaching a hospital? Was she conscious and with a nice nurse or ambulance man or lady holding her hand, giving her support, and keeping her from feeling frightened till the end?

She knew she would have to face the facts, sooner rather than later, and needed to prepare herself for the worst, but Cora still felt too numb.

She accepted a cup of tea from her mother and decided that what she really wanted to do, was to be at home, to be with some of Belle's things and to go and lie on her bed and smell her, find something that really reminded her of her beautiful daughter.

Cora needed to leave, but she was also aware of her mother's pain. She tried to explain why she needed to go home, and asked Belinda, whether she wanted to come with her.

Her mother was surprised to be asked and quickly accepted, as if suddenly, every second with Cora had become incredibly precious, and hoped it would help make up for all those lost years of brief and stern communications.

But as they sat in the car, Cora turned round and facing Belinda said:

'Is Raith my father?'

Belinda's mouth just dropped open. This was the last thing she had been expecting. Anything but this.

'If this is going to be the worst day of my life,' Cora said, 'I want to know about the things you've been keeping from me, and I want this avalanche to hit me now, I want all the pain at the same time.'

A moment later Cora added: 'That is what I had come to see you about, before Mark called. I want to know, and now it is even more important for me to understand, and to be able to let my children know, if their grandfather, is someone they have never met. I can't cope with all the details, but I just want to know.'

Belinda didn't know where to start.

She hadn't been prepared for this and she felt so lost and drenched by Belle's death that she wished Raith could be there now, with them, to help her explain. She had never expected Cora would find out about her past, and certainly never imagined she would be confronted by her, in this manner.

Belinda and Edward had protected the girls and were sure they would never come to find out about their biological father. That had been the deal.

Of course, 'the deal' hadn't quite worked out as they had planned…and that was her fault, and her fault alone.

'Yes, he is. And Laura's as well,' said Belinda.

'But before you say anything, Edward couldn't have children. He told me before we married, expecting I would flee; I had lost Raith, or so I thought, and I was very conscious that the love I felt for Edward was of a different kind, a new kind. I was very young… but I wanted to have my own children, so rather than run the risk of losing me, he proposed I have a child by another as long as nobody ever found out.'

'He loved you like he would have done if you were his. More in fact probably, because he was so aware of his physical shortcomings, that the gift of a family with a child was something he had only ever dreamt of.'

'He was the most generous man I have ever met.' Belinda took a deep breath and decided to go on as Cora sat listening in silence.

'He never knew about Raith. He knew he existed, but purely as far as the man I had loved before him, and he suspected he may have been your father, but he didn't really want to know.

He didn't believe I may still be in love with him.'

Belinda carried on, 'I think he thought I may have arranged to see him again, only with the purpose of getting pregnant, rather than choosing a stranger.

'I never gave Edward any reason to suspect that I was in love with someone else, because I made him happy… at least until Robin died.

'I know you will find that difficult to understand but your father's…

'Edward's and my relationship, was, by and large, a very happy one. I had huge respect and pride in him, and he would have done anything for us. The love I felt for him was of a very good kind and I miss him. He was strong in a way that made me feel protected.

'What Raith and I had, have, is altogether different, and difficult to explain and has led to much pain, but it also made my marriage survive. When Robin Browne died, it hit Helena extremely hard because of course he was her first child.

'Their eldest daughter was adopted, as initially, Helena didn't think she could have children. And Raith still had you both, and their youngest son, Peter. After Helena had a breakdown, Raith decided that his loyalties must be to her, first, and we said our goodbyes.

'Within a few months without him, the void and hollow his absence caused became so evident to me, that I found living with Edward a terrible struggle, and we both became deeply unhappy. I regret that so very much, as your father, the one who loved you and brought you up, did not deserve such punishment from me. I would give anything to be able to relive those last ten years again, and make him happy.' She paused, but then carried on, as all this information suddenly started flooding out of her, as if it couldn't be stopped now…

'He had done everything to give us a lovely life, and never asked anything of me, apart from my affection and respect. Our relationship wasn't intimate and we both accepted that, but it was so many other special things.

'When I got pregnant the second time with Laura, Edward just thought I had had a desperate longing for a second child, and we never spoke about the how… That is how much he loved me,

'I am so sorry my darling for everything. For hiding all this from you; for blaming you in some way, while I was going through the pain of being apart from Raith, I was very stubborn, tricky, and distant, and unappreciative of all you have helped me with. You, far more than your sister, reminded me of Raith, every time I looked at you. When Edward died, I really felt that my life had been pretty hopeless. I had hurt people and, ultimately, hadn't felt truly happy at all. I went into a shell, to protect myself I think, and may be others too. I found out that Raith had moved here, only a couple of weeks ago, and today we met for the second time, to talk, and it was good to do so. I don't know what made you suspect you may be his daughter, but you can tell me that in your own time… not today.'

Cora wondered whether any of what her mother had just told her had actually, 'gone in.' Would she even remember any of it by tomorrow? There was no space left in her head for reason, surely, not after what had happened to Belle? Where was the reason in her death?

She held her mother's hand, for a moment, started the car,

and drove off in silence. This was starting to feel completely surreal. Her daughter had just died, and she had just learned that the person she believed to be her father, was not.

18

The next few days were an apocalyptic blur for Cora.

A deep fog engulfed her, with moments which alternated between private desperation and robotic efficiency. She had started the process of letting people know about the accident, then had travelled to London to see Belle's body. To see her precious girl, just lying there, seemingly at peace, but horribly pale and motionless, had been the hardest thing she had ever experienced. She had thrown herself into putting together the funeral, with hymns, readings and poems, chosen carefully with the help of her boys.

But although Cora went about executing these tasks in her usual, firm and efficient way, which, under these sad circumstances, felt like the only thing to do, she felt frozen inside. Numb.

When she could allow herself a few minutes alone, she would succumb to a deluge of emotions and feelings of complete and utter despair and tears, which she seemed unable to control.

Cora had been good at managing problems in the past, efficient and orderly, but this was something she could never have foreseen. She tried to deal with things in a business-like manner, as she found that to be the only way she could cope, without collapsing. She wondered whether this was how others also coped when a tragedy of this magnitude happened and whether that was why, at times, people seem quite cold and unemotional at the funerals of close relatives, and the days that preceded it...

And because Mark had never been good at taking decisions, Cora found herself having to organise everything.

He relied on her, even now, to do this, and she quietly resented him. She resented him over the pain she knew he must be feeling, and she was not proud of that, but she couldn't stop it.

He seemed incapable of any opinion with regards to the funeral and she wished he wasn't around at all in some way...

Cora felt that, in fact, had Mark not been there, it would have been easier on her. She knew she was wrong to think ill of him; he was Belle's father and was suffering just as much as she was, but she felt so desperately alone, that she didn't really know how to behave any differently.

Belinda had been supportive, but Cora hadn't had the time to consider all she had said to her the day Belle had died, and it seemed so unimportant now.

Cora found selecting the readings, and hymns for the church service, the most difficult of tasks.

A responsibility which she carried out with such sadness. How could she even start to imagine what Belle would have liked her send-off to be like.

Cora had no idea what Belle's favourite hymn might have been, or of a reading which she may have particularly liked, and she had asked Francis and Ludo, but they didn't know, either.

It seemed to her that this ignorance of hers was like yet another punishment from someone above. Of course, nobody that young would think of preparing for death, but maybe the whole idea of dying - ironically, what she herself feared the most - should be confronted at secondary school, in a more extensive and wholesome way.

It could be discussed openly, with every person given the opportunity of writing down what they would like their funeral to be about. Teachers could make this into an engaging and light-hearted journey, which would take the edge off the subject of not being on earth any more, whatever time of life that happened.

Then those left behind would have something 'to go by', and know that their loved ones had planned the whole thing.

Cora was just trying to occupy her brain with some constructive, but no doubt, absolutely, unrealistic thoughts. Why have funerals anyway… who are they really for… she reflected.

The day in question started strangely, as Cora slipped into the simple, navy dress she had chosen, and realised that it was too small.

She couldn't believe she had been so foolish as not to try it on before, but she had just assumed that, with all the upset over Belle, and stress before that, she had probably lost weight. She angrily opened her cupboard, and quickly decided on another navy ensemble.

She didn't want to wear black. It would just be too depressing and make her feel worse. So, she pulled out an old skirt and a long sleeve navy silk shirt.

The sun was particularly warm.

Belle would have loved that, and Skye seemed to show great excitement at the amount of people coming in and out of the house. Such an anti-climax, but a welcome one nevertheless; her dog had never had so much attention.

It's quite extraordinary what quiet relief and distraction a domestic animal, can offer to those people who struggle to look you in the eye, while expressing their condolences.

All had gone according to plan in the church and Cora felt proud of her boys, and how strong they had been and had made her feel, holding her hand through the whole service, apart from when they had stood up, to go and speak about their sister. Ludo had written a piece about Belle's life, and memories of when they were small, with silly events that had happened, and had done so well, making the congregation laugh more than once, which had helped.

Francis had read two beautiful poems chosen from a book he had found on Belle's bedside table, both of which had been incredibly lovely and touching.

Amanda Thompson, one of Belle's greatest and oldest friends, had also spoken about her so beautifully.

Mark had done one of the readings, with one of Francis's friends, who had briefly dated Belle, reading the other.

As the coffin was taken out of the church, Cora found herself unconsciously looking for Raith in the crowd. She wondered whether he might have managed to attend, to say goodbye to a granddaughter he hadn't even known, but she couldn't see him.

As she walked out into the bright light, the sun shone on Belle's coffin. Cora, noticed Jill coming towards her, and felt slightly faint at the idea of having to speak to her right now. She didn't think she could quite cope with the effort of doing so, because although so kind, Jill was rather 'full-on' at the best of times.

Cora could feel Ludo's body just gently leaning into her from behind, as people were slowly making their way out of the church. She suddenly turned round to face him, and whispered to him, and to Mark standing behind him, that she would like to get into her car, which was due to follow the hearse, as quickly as possible.

She didn't want to face anyone just yet.

Francis could stay behind to talk to people who had decided not to come to the burial and follow on in a while.

Belle wasn't going to be buried here, but by Edward's grave in Pouston, in the village the children had always known as 'where granny and gramps lived.'

Belle would have liked that, Cora, was sure of it. She had adored her grandfather. The man Belle knew as her grandfather, Cora thought with sadness, and a little bitterness.

As the door of her car was about to be closed by Mark, she suddenly thought she saw Nicholas, standing in the large crowd that had now come out of the church.

She gasped in surprise, and Ludo asked her whether she was alright, but it was too late for her to move towards him now.

She hadn't thought about Nicholas, not since the moment she had received the phone call about Belle's tragic accident, and was totally taken aback by his presence here.

She hadn't expected to ever see him again in fact.

As they reached Belinda's village and the churchyard, she found herself hoping he may come for the burial. But he didn't, and Cora found she really wished he had made it, which was ridiculous in the circumstances. What did it matter anyway ?

Especially at a time when the only important things were saying her final goodbyes to Belle and being with the family.

Many people Cora knew from the village, came back to the cottage, and many of Belle's London and university friends came too.

Cora had organised a tea, with her typical efficiency, helped by Kitty, who had stayed the night before at a B&B. Both Kitty and Carol, had been absolutely brilliant and had brought lots of food from London. As Cora walked through her own front door, the house was already full. It was like walking into someone else's home, such an odd feeling.

She slipped into her business mode, though all she actually wanted to do was to run to her bedroom, fall into her bed, and not leave it again for days. It didn't feel like her cottage at all, her nest, with all these people in it.

Cora felt, weirdly, as if she was the stranger there.

Even the serving plates, with the finger food that was been handed around, were unfamiliar to her… she didn't recognise the pattern. There were little yellow flowers on it, she didn't like it at all.

She would never have chosen it.

For a moment, Cora thought she might just scream, she could frighten everyone away. She knew she was being petty, and disrespectful, and had to pull herself together.

The grieving process of losing a child when divorced, let alone when not even having a partner, was going to be a hard and lonely journey for her.

She hadn't found her peace with Belinda yet; not enough to be able to allow for that genuine and natural mother/daughter closeness that could have really helped and supported her. She wasn't particularly close to Laura, and she had to be strong for Francis and Ludo. Especially for them.

During the first couple of days after Belle's accident, she had recognised a few of the feelings for Mark, she hadn't contemplated for many years. It seemed to Cora a reminder of why she had fallen for him; but they were very short-lived. She soon saw through the person she had left long ago. And why.

Cora suddenly noticed someone she didn't recognise, feeding Skye half a sandwich which they had obviously decided they didn't like and instead of letting it go, Cora stormed forward and bossily asked them not to do it again.

Not her finest moment.

But then they hadn't just lost their daughter, she thought. She recognised the person to be one of the volunteers in the village charity shop, which she had visited so often, and she suddenly felt awful for having been abrupt.

She looked at Mark, who was standing in the corner of the sitting room, drinking a beer and laughing with someone, she didn't recognise from behind. How odd she thought, but she accepted that everyone reacts differently to loss and grief, trying to relax now that the funeral was over, was obviously his way. She could feel resentment building up inside her; she begrudged the fact that he had someone to go back to, to console him, to hold and hug and kiss him.

She knew this was wrong of her, very wrong, especially today.

Again, she felt a strange longing to see Nicholas, but he hadn't come to the house either. Cora started wondering whether she might have just imagined seeing him outside the church.

This thought kept niggling at her… then she suddenly remembered that he had been due to leave for Africa a few days before, so it couldn't have been him.

What a fool she had been to think he would have cancelled his departure to Africa to come to the funeral of her daughter, whom he had never met.

Cora hadn't slept for more than three hours per night for the past week. She thought of Helena Browne, one person she knew who had suffered in just the same way, in very similar circumstances; neither she, nor Raith had come today, which must be because of Belinda.

Suddenly someone caught her arm from behind, holding it firmly, but gently. It was Jill. She hugged her and for some reason they both burst into tears. Nothing unusual about this, apart from the fact that Cora had managed to hold back her tears, all day, and had promised herself not to start crying until everyone had left as she feared that once started, she would find it hard to stop.

Jill wasn't anyone she had allowed herself to be overly emotional with in the past. Straight and honest yes, but not emotional.

Somehow though Jill felt very strong and warm and safe. She was now looking straight at Cora and said:

'I am here, and I want you to know that I don't want you spending one second alone once Francis, Ludo and Mark return to London, you must come and stay until you feel stronger.'

It was such a sweet thing to offer, and Cora truly appreciated it, but at the same time she was longing to be alone, with her own thoughts. Probably the worst thing she should be doing right now, but nevertheless she longed for peace, space and time after the last week. She needed that, so to take in the dramatic events that had followed her trip to Ireland, trip which seemed so silly and futile now.

She felt so weak, both physically and mentally, so much so that she worried she wouldn't have the strength to take Skye for her walk. I wonder, she thought, if a dog feels the grief that surrounds it…

How could her life recover from this? She must find a way, for the sake of the boys.

It was her duty and commitment to them, as their mother. To be for them all she would have been, had Belle still been alive.

She must. Absolutely must, and that thought would bring her the strength she needed to carry on, but she just couldn't quite yet.

On Tuesday morning, Mark drove Ludo back to London. Francis left that evening by train, although very reluctantly; he knew his mother well and could feel her desperate loss in a way only he and, ironically, Belle could have done. Leaving Cora alone in the cottage didn't seem like the right thing to do but they discussed it, and decided together that she really wanted some time alone. Even if it was just a few days.

Mark was longing to get back to his girlfriend, and had just been awfully difficult over the past two days, and Ludo, although he would never have said, was desperate to get back to Bee and the normality of his usual routine… flat, gym, office, out to the pub with the boys etc. Cora didn't think Ludo was, in any form, grieving less than any of them, not deep down, but he had a great way of putting difficult issues to one side; always had done, even as a child.

Francis had to get back to work but had offered to take time off so that Cora wouldn't be alone. His flat mate, Harry, had been incredibly kind and had offered his bedroom to Cora so she could stay in London, near Francis, for a few weeks, but this was not what Cora wished. Deep down she just wanted to grieve alone, here.

In many ways, it was good that Francis and Belle and Ludo hadn't seen each other with any great regularity since prep school. They had been to different boarding schools so hadn't really spent much time with each other apart from during the holidays, and had always had a very separate set of friends, because of the three year gap between each of them.

Cora felt helpless and exhausted.

She was lacking any energy, and even the smallest of tasks seemed humongous to her.

Today was going to be the first day she would have taken Skye out for a walk on her own, since Belle's death, and she wasn't entirely sure she could cope.

What if she met someone when she was out? One of the neighbours, or someone from the village… they were bound to ask her questions, and she just wasn't ready for that yet. The telephone rang and Cora recognised Jill's number. She felt her strength wash away, and even the energy to deal with her well-meaning neighbour, abandoned her…

She sat deeper into the familiar armchair and fell asleep.

19

Cora was woken by gentle knocks on the kitchen window. She opened her eyes and it took her a few seconds to focus, until Nicholas's face became too clear and vivid, to believe it may be another hallucination.

She stared at him from her seat for a full minute before leaping up with surprise. She walked towards the glass door and unlocked it. Nicholas came in and before either of them could say anything, he took her into his arms.

Cora let her weight fall completely in his embrace.

She looked terrible, felt terrible and she was beyond caring that Nicholas would see her like this. She started crying so loudly that he couldn't think of what to do, so he kissed her gently on her trembling lips.

In most situations this could, would, have been regarded as awful timing, bad taste and in fact probably seen as taking full advantage of her misery, mainly to serve his own physical longing to get close to her. But somehow, it was everything but.

Initially, Cora had pulled away, confused by the moment and her own emotions, but then, she allowed Nicholas to kiss her again and she kissed him back and this time, with warmth. Nicholas was still holding most of her weight in his arms, he walked her back to her favourite armchair and sat her tenderly in it again, as if she were a small child. One, who is ill with a fever, and needs much care. He knelt on the floor holding her hands and kissing them whispering: 'I am here, I am here now.'

Cora looked into his eyes and saw a man she now felt she had known all her life.

'What are you doing here?' she whispered...

'Jill called me as soon as she heard... and I wanted to be here for you. I wasn't entirely sure coming over was going to give you any comfort at all, in fact I feared quite the opposite after the way I must have seemed to you in Ireland, but I just felt I needed to see you before leaving. To hold you in my arms and to make sure you were not alone and... well the rest doesn't really matter just now. I hope you don't mind me being here like this; during such a terribly sad time when you need your family around you... I am sorry. I shouldn't have come.'

Nicholas was looking deeply into her eyes now and continued...

'When Jill called to say Belle had died, somehow so much of what we had talked about in Ireland came crashing down on me.'

He paused then added 'I hadn't wanted to listen to you. I felt scared that I would never see you again, that I had missed the opportunity to tell you how I actually felt. I know that what I do, and have done for years, is to grieve for someone who is in fact not dead. I felt ashamed, foolish about the fact that I had hidden behind this feeling for so long. And you were right. It has stopped me living my life, and you are now in a situation where you have truly lost your daughter and have a right to grieve for her, while I absolutely do not.'

Nicholas continued to explain, 'Selina may not be with me, or ever will be, in a way that I would truly wish, but she is alive and well. I am so sorry for hurting you, and for your loss.'

Nicholas added: 'I was just terrified of anything changing the way my life has been for so long, and when Belle died, I knew how scared you must be feeling about life, and your future without her in it.'

Nicholas stayed the night, in Ludo's bedroom and although he would have loved to share Cora's bed, she felt totally unable to delve into her intimate self.

She welcomed the tenderness of his hugs and even his occasional kisses but couldn't bring herself to go any further. Not because she didn't fancy him, but because it just didn't feel like the right time or the right place.

Cora wasn't even sure whether there would be a right time or a right place again. It was all too soon.

She felt that Belle deserved all her love and attention, even if dead and to give love to anyone else, other than Francis and Ludo, was being disloyal to all three.

Cora knew this wasn't a realistic view of life, but that was all she could cope with.

Nicholas left the next afternoon as he had to finish off the last few arrangements before leaving for Africa, and Cora had been genuinely upset to see him go but at the same time, she knew it was for the best.

He had been wonderful while there, had cooked for her and held her. His kindness, understanding and gentleness, had gone well beyond anything she had derived from her first meetings with him, and certainly her latest visit to Ireland. But she couldn't consider anything beyond friendship now, and he had a project that would take him a long way away, for at least six months.

Cora and Nicholas promised to stay in touch, and she was

grateful that she had someone outside her inner family and closest friends who she might be able to chat to now and again.

She thought about Mark. It had been a hard few days to get through and she knew she had not made his time there any easier.

She was regretting it now, and she would call him later, before he returned home to his girlfriend, to apologise. She had found it hard to share what was her special, and personal space, her house, with the person she least wanted to have in it.

Everything she had done with the cottage, all its belongings and furnishings, were part of what was most precious to her, and had been through the years from her childhood. Since the breakup of her marriage, they had become hugely significant.

Thinking about her past brought to mind Sebastian, and Cora remembered he hadn't been in touch. She hadn't given him a thought for the past week. That was, in itself, rather healthy, whatever the circumstances. It did cross her mind that he may not have heard the news of Belle's death, but she decided not to phone him. He had never taken a huge interest in her children, so to expect him to do so now, would be unrealistic and hardly necessary.

She didn't wish for his sympathy. As she was about to text Mark, a message from Ludo came through. Her youngest son did not tend to message his mother a great deal at all, unless he wanted to come home, so Cora was a little anxious to see his name at the top of the text.

Was he ok? Had she spent enough time talking to him? She suddenly worried she hadn't taken the boys feelings of grief into consideration enough, and had let them return to London, when they might not have been totally ready to go…

By the time she had read the content, she had to sit down, as what Ludo was implying certainly came as a surprise.

He had been offered a position in the company's Sydney office, about two weeks ago, and had not given his answer yet. When Belle had died, he felt he couldn't possibly leave Cora on her own, even though his visits home were hardly that frequent, but Cora felt that he was basically putting this dilemma in her court. It wouldn't be for more than three years, his message said, and would be a great career move. Why had he not spoken about this in the last few days? May be he had been frightened to, thought Cora.

She also wondered about Bee, his girlfriend. How would she feel? But the answer to that came in the next text. Bee would go with him and get a job out there for the duration of his. It sounded as if his mind was already made up, but what Ludo really wished for, was Cora's blessing.

She phoned and told him that he must go and that she agreed that it was a wonderful opportunity for him. It had come at a good time, and there seemed no reason to remain around her or his father, as they would hardly be very good company for a while. He was young and had his whole life ahead of him, and he must live it to the full.

The moment Cora had ended her conversation with her youngest son, she burst into tears. She knew, in her heart, that she had said all the right things to Ludo, but she was still feeling so fragile and vulnerable, that she felt this had landed on her plate as the last straw.

She already felt so alone, and utterly lost. She was in many ways losing a daughter and a son in the space of ten days.

The little strength left within her, told her that self-pity would bring her no peace or joy, and that she must somehow survive this. She must feel pleased for Ludo, but she just didn't quite know how to…

She had relied on all her children's love and support in the past, especially during the breakups of her previous relationships; Belle's in particular, not only because she was a woman, but because she was the one who was most like Cora and now, with only Francis left in London, she knew that a great hollow would soon be felt.

Deep down, Cora knew full well that her neediness was mainly due to the lack of love that comes with a strong personal and intimate relationship, and the continuity of it. Relying on such love from one's own children, especially once they are grown up, was not the right way to go; not in the long term. But that was easier said than done.

She was going to miss Belle terribly. Her tenderness and affection, had been part of Cora's life, nearly on a daily basis, for years, as they communicated a lot on WhattsApp. While the boys tended to take a while to reply to her messages, Belle had always loved her mother's messages, and would always get in touch soon after Cora had written to her. Even if it was just to send a heart or smiley emoji. She had been so sensitive and understanding of her mother's ups and downs, and although Belle had been the middle child, she had always shown great maturity.

Cora had confided in her daughter in the past few years in a way she would have struggled to do with Francis and Ludo, probably out of fear, that they would have been rather reluctant to listen to her problems.

Or maybe it was that Cora didn't mind somehow showing her vulnerability towards the same sex and wanted to, very much, show a strong front with her boys.

Now, she not only needed to pull through this, but to make something of what was left of her life. The question was, what could she rescue out of this desperate situation?

She tried to think ahead, in three years' time; Ludo would be back in the UK, back in his London office, quite possibly engaged to Bee and living not too far away again.

Would they get engaged in Australia and may be even get married out there? That would be fine, as long as they didn't decide to settle there, she hoped.

The next day Cora woke up and took an unexpected, but nevertheless firm, decision about the path ahead of her.

20

Cora decided that she would sell her cottage.

She knew now, that being alone so often, gave her loneliness too much scope to lay down its roots. And, at the cottage, isolation had become part of a daily routine, in a way that she had felt she had often needed, in between break-ups, but not anymore.

She had been so independent, especially over the last year, and had enjoyed the privacy of her own surroundings, and the feelings of safety and contentment, but the location was too remote for what Cora had in mind. Cora was looking at her life, with different eyes now. Sad, but determined ones.

She felt that the right recipe, was not necessarily about losing her independence, but gaining the opportunity to be able to walk out of her home, and be surrounded by people and things to do.

With Belle's loss and Ludo's news of his imminent move to Australia, Cora knew this was for the best.

She wanted to feel closer to Francis and to her best friends, Kitty and Carol. She was going to move to London.

She secretly also knew that life in her cottage, now, would aggravate her mild depression and she was going to take this big leap of faith in herself, as it was all very well going to the odd supper party once a month, and Jill had been more than friendly, but Cora now longed for people, noise, life, colour, and the hustle and bustle of streets, squares and parks.

Skye of course came to her mind and how she might take to such a change of life-style, but Cora knew that as long as she was with her, Skye would manage; she would buy a little flat with a garden.

The thought of moving suddenly made her smile. A smile which she could feel on her lips for the first time for many weeks. This decision suddenly flooded her mind with one thousand things to do, which was exactly what she needed.

It was the first positive step she had taken for some time.

Cora got a note pad and a pen and started making a list of everything she had to do to get the ball rolling. The first thought, after Skye of course, was about her family, then her close friends, and what their reaction may or not be.

Interestingly enough, probably for the first time in her life, this didn't fill her with doubt or fear, as so often announcing a change in her circumstances had in the past, especially when ending relationships. She felt more that a certain curiosity, and a lot of apprehension, would come from her mother. Belinda could hardly say she would miss her. Since discovering that Raith and Belinda had been in touch, Cora felt far less guilty about thinking of only herself, in this decision.

Yes, this was to be Cora's resolve and one she made one hundred percent for Cora and her happiness.

The fact that she would end up seeing far more of Francis and, in three years Ludo as well, was a major part of her decision. As well as being close to Kitty and Carol.

Cora sensed, that moving to London, would no doubt result in her missing some of the benefits of village life, and especially her garden, but she also recognised, that being around people she loved, was far more important now. She felt she was being very honest with her feelings, and possibly very brave too, as this was a big step to take at her age.

Cora drove to Belinda's the next day, and was a little surprised to find that Raith's car was, again, parked outside her house. There were no traces of wishing to hide the fact this time. She had probably made far more out of their friendship now that it needed to be, but nevertheless, she wondered whether Helena was aware of his whereabouts.

Cora could have easily have turned away and come back another time, but she was so caught up in this flow of activity in her mind, that she just wished to tick this particular box off her list, and get on with all the other tasks she had assigned herself.

She didn't wish to find obstacles so early on in her new venture. She quickly reprimanded herself for using such a term as an obstacle, to describe telling her mother about her decision. Announcing her intentions to Belinda, should surely count for more than a tick off a to-do list, but nevertheless she certainly didn't feel strong enough to put the visit off to another time, just because Raith was there.

He was her father after all, so in fact, she suddenly saw this as a perfect opportunity, to kill two birds with one stone.

She turned the handle of the front door announcing herself rather more loudly that usual, but in fact had to call a few more times, before getting an answer.

Her mother and Raith seemed to be in deep conversation at the end of the garden and didn't seem in the least surprised to see her there. Both came up and kissed her hello and Cora felt slightly uncomfortable, purely because she had never seen them together like this, so was a little stuck with what to say next.

Cora had forgotten to ask Belinda, whether Raith knew that

she was now aware that Laura and herself were his daughters…

The answer to that came very soon after the thought had crossed her mind.

Raith held out his hands to her, and Belinda rested hers on both of them. He looked deeply into Cora's eyes and just said: 'I am so sorry, for everything.'

Cora felt confused at how to reply, so just allowed herself a gentle smile and pulled her hands back to her side. This was just enough to let Raith know, that his daughter, wasn't prepared to listen to another lengthy explanation of the past, not yet anyway.

Cora needed to assimilate so much right now… her grief still so raw after Belle's death.

She had come to see Belinda for a specific reason, and didn't particularly feel like having her impetus derailed. She broke the news of her wish to move to London, as soon as they stepped back into Belinda's kitchen.

After an initial look of bewilderment, Belinda gave her full support to her daughter, in such a spontaneous way, that Cora actually was left believing her mother was genuinely thrilled for her.

Belinda was pleased for Cora, but was this guided more by Belinda's guilt over her affair with Raith, than genuine happiness for her daughter? Cora wondered…

Nevertheless, Cora allowed her mother to hug and kiss her, although sharing this closeness with her, still felt rather strained and weird.

She knew in that moment, that Belinda wouldn't be playing a very big role in her new life in London.

Cora was heading for a less complicated, more genuine and

happier time, surrounded by people she trusted and respected.

She wanted to move on, to grieve for her daughter, to start putting herself and her health first.

Belinda and Raith could look after each other.

After all, wasn't that what they'd always done? Cora said her goodbyes and drove home, feeling stronger and more positive.

Skye welcomed her home with excitement, especially as she had not been taken for her walk yet. She had never quite learned not to jump up onto Cora's lap, when wishing to share her happiness, but today, Cora found herself encouraging this.

She grabbed her coat, closed her front door behind her with vigour, and started walking through the path that lead from her garden gate towards the park to the west of the village.

While Skye eagerly pulled on her lead, Cora started telling her loyal friend about all the adventures that lay ahead of them; even though one of these couldn't include a dog, as it was going to mean a long trip, too far away and too hot for Skye.

A trip to Africa sometime, in the not too distant future. Just for a couple of weeks.

But London must come first and a new home for them both was a priority, and they would look for that together.

Very soon. In fact, Cora told Skye that she would call the local estate agents in the morning, to discuss a valuation on the cottage, before putting it up for sale.

For the first time in her life, Cora felt she was starting to understand the meaning of the term 'letting go'. And she liked the sound of it.

THE END

Acknowledgements

My thanks go to my other half, Vere, for his love and support and for believing in me. To my children Joe and Guy, for putting up with me and for sharing the enthusiasm and excitement in writing my first novel. To the rest of my lovely family for their support in this venture; to Willie without whom this book would never have taken off; to my brother Roberto, author, poet and photographer.

Huge thanks to all the team at The Conrad Press for publishing this, my first book, and in particular the brilliant and inspiring James Essinger. I have learnt so much from him. I am grateful beyond words to Francesca Garratt, not only for being my editor but also for her advice, support and patient ear. Her guidance was invaluable. Thank you to Charlotte Mouncey for her generosity, and understanding so well what I wished to achieve with my book cover.

Last but not least, my love and thanks go to Elsa, who was there during all my writing, keeping me company and constantly nudging me to take her for a walk.